THE DISTRICTS

An Unorganized Tale About Organized Crime

JARED CARRILLO

To Enrique

Father to myself and my two sisters.

Thank you for the inspiration that will follow me forever and then eventually follow my kids. You will always be missed. I hope I'm making you proud.

1956-2018

"Do you know where you are?"

(Special Thanks)

My sisters: Giselle Casey and Skyelar Carrillo for the years of fun adventures and a bunch of lectures that are now paying off.

My Mom: Faith Drennen for being the best mom ever.

Six: John Drennen for taking care of me for these years.

Matt and Aimee Fennell for letting me into their home **ALL** of the time.

Ian (Max) Fennell for being a big brother to me through these first two years of high school, and a big brother for the rest of my life even though I have to make sure he stays out of trouble.

Jacob (Jake) Fennell for reading all of my stories and making the funniest memories ever with Sammet.

Aidan Charletta for pushing me to write this book. You have been my biggest supporter.

Cesar (Sam) Aguirre for the FaceTimes and the late night toast we make at fight night. You are the smartest guy I know who does the dumbest things with me all of the time. You're a fighter.

Nicholas (Nick) Lechwar for the memories we make every time we hang out.

Mallory Frattle for sticking with me after all of my downfalls. Thanks for being my best friend.

Antonio (Antwon) Alicea for livening up every fight night and going a little too far sometimes.

Will Sammet for making me piss my pants at every restaurant we go to with Jake.

Noah Ferrizzi for giving me the name of my protagonist and the best summer ever.

Andrew Kyles for making me laugh even under stress. For example: ketchup roulette.

To all of you, I thank you from the bottom of my heart. You made this happen.

The Districts

An Unorganized Tale About Organized Crime

©2021 Jared Carrillo

print ISBN: 978-1-66781-980-8

CONTENTS

Chapter 1: Meet The Santinos   1

Chapter 2: 'Twas the Night Before Christmas...   11

Chapter 3: Business Trip   23

Chapter 4: BAM!   35

Chapter 5: Balcony Blitz   43

Chapter 6: White Stuff   57

Chapter 7: Let's Settle This   80

Chapter 8: Enter Sinful and Dying   107

Chapter 9: The Abruzzo Deal   121

Chapter 10: Sincerely, Noah   139

CHAPTER 1:

MEET THE SANTINOS

Welcome to the business. Once you go in, you don't go out.

District: a district is a branch of a group partnership involved in a different kind of organized crime than the mafia. However, some of the same rules apply. Districts and mafia families don't compete; they do their own thing, but they don't associate at all. Districts are more understanding and fair than the mafia. There is no chain of command, everybody pretty much makes the same amount unless they have side gigs, which are frowned upon. Initiation differs: in the mafia, you take The Oath of Omertá, but in the district business you just take your fellow district heads out for dinner. In the mafia, there is one boss per family. In the districts, there can be several.

I n 1949, Raymond Santino had a tough choice to make. On the one hand, he had a meeting with the head of the Russo District, which would be a huge turning point for his own district. On the other hand, his wife was about to give birth to twins on the same night. His wife, Sofia, gave birth to two young boys, Leonardo and Noah, without her husband holding her hand. Raymond decided to let his associates know that he prioritizes them, so he decided to spend the night eating a T-Bone with the Russo District.

By the end of the dinner, he was a father and co-founder of Russo Santino. This is what is referred to as "the historic decision".

Russo Santino was a restaurant owned by Raymond and Henry Russo, mainly used for money laundering. It became one of the most popular restaurants in Manhattan. Money was coming in every night, which made for a perfect cover-up.

By the time Leonardo and Noah were celebrating their tenth birthday, Raymond's hair was turning gray. *Maybe I'm getting too old for this*, Raymond would think to himself. He'd look at his two boys playing around in the yard, and he'd pray that one day they will be able to inherit the business just like he did. The only problem is that he doesn't want to leave the business behind.

Raymond always favored Leonardo, who he would call Leo. He made it evident, which ticked Sofia off. Leonardo, even at his young age, knew that if he kissed his father's ass just enough that it would pay off one day. At the time, he had no clue that Raymond was the head of a vast criminal district. He just knew that his dad had money and that his money would go to him if he kept it up.

Noah was never too upset about his dad's lack of love towards him. He loved his father very much and would always think that he was the wisest man alive. So in his mind, when his dad loved Leo over him, he felt it was the right choice.

Leo and Noah had a good relationship. As time would pass, they'd have more and more fights. They were never for a good reason. It would be about who would have a better shot at scoring the cute girls they see. They went to quite a few at district meetings Raymond would make them attend. Raymond's friends and associates would have their kids tag along if they were going to Russo Santino, but of course the kids never knew.

By the time Leo and Noah were turning eighteen, Raymond knew it was time to tell them about the district. He claimed that they both would take over when he retires. It would be the first duo for any district in history. After those years of loyalty to his father, Leo was hurt that he was only rewarded with a partnership instead of the boss.

The Santino District has four partnerships: Russo, Alfredo, Colombo, and Bruno. The Santino District was a distribution organization, Raymond would have clients that he would attend to. Henry Russo did many deliveries for Raymond. Antonio Alfredo and Raymond were as tight as brothers but kept it professional when it came to business. Alfredo owned a pizza joint and would use it for money laundering and store any possessions Raymond felt he needed to secure. Luca Bruno's District wasn't one that you would use daily. His district did many things, but Raymond exclusively used him for hits. Luca's team had a beautiful record of never missing a shot. James Colombo deals with narcotics, but never really attends any of the meetings.

Colombo would store his narcotics in Alfredo's store, and would supply them to Raymond whenever he would make a deal. Raymond would ship the narcotics in Russo's trucks.

Eventually, 1978 approached, and Raymond knew it was time to step down, which he hated to do. His wife was dead, and all of his hair was gray. He loved the business more than he loved Sofia. He would've even done it for free. The only reason why he didn't stick around a little longer was that Henry passed down the business to his son, just like Luca and Antonio. All of the heads were fresh faces to Raymond.

Before Raymond could step down, he had to be sure that the district was in good hands with all of his heart. He decided to give Leo and Noah a test run.

PRESENT DAY:

After a terrible gig, Leo gathers with three heads: Marco Russo, Mario Alfredo, and Robert Bruno. He wants to reassure that their partnership is not in jeopardy due to his and Noah's first gig.

"I'm fresh. You all were fresh at one point," Leo says. "The gig didn't severely affect any of you guys."

"Leo, it's not about that," Mario starts. "The fact of the matter is you had a shot and blew it. Now, I'm not one to judge you off on your first impression. With that said, I don't speak for all of us."

Leo rubs his forehead in frustration. Ever since he learned about the business, he couldn't help but love it. Leo wants the money, but that's not what's keeping him in the game. He wants pride and respect. He wants to keep the Santino legacy.

"Where's your brother? Shouldn't your brother be here for this?" Marco asks.

Leo sighs and says, "He absolutely should be here. I agree. But, he has personal matters to attend to, unfortunately. I speak for the both of us tonight."

"Look, at the end of the day, I'm not going to conclude our partnership because of the failure," Marco says. "It's your father that I think you should be worrying about."

Leo looks at Marco in the eyes and assures, "My relationship with him should be the least of your concerns. My father is extremely fond of me. What do you think will happen?"

"Well, your father weighed in on the situation with my father," Mario says. "He asked for a recommendation on who should run his district."

Leo's jaw drops down to hell. The message was more shocking to him than the JFK assassination. "Are you yanking my chain? Is he trying to recruit from outside the family? Why wouldn't he say this to Noah or me?"

They shrug their shoulders and continue to dig into their meals. Henrietta, the hostess, comes up to him and says, "Mr. Santino, you have a call."

"Is it my father? And I thought I told you to hold all of my calls." Leo barks at his hostess.

"My mistake, sir. It's your brother. Sounds urgent."

"He knows that I'm in this meeting that he should be in, too. Tell him I'll give him a ring in an hour or so."

Robert says, "Take it. We don't mind."

Leo sighs and smiles at his fellow district heads. He gets up from the table and walks over to the hostess stand to answer the phone. "You fuckin' prick. Where's your brain?"

On the other end, Noah is on the couch as he holds his phone to his ear with his left hand and a gun to his mistress's head with his right. "I need you to come over here."

"Where do you get off? Here I am, saving our asses while you are doing whatever the hell you are doing. These men aren't too happy with us, and to be honest, I'm not too happy with us either. The last thing I'm going to do is leave the meeting."

"You'll regret not stopping by. I cannot stress this enough." Noah begs.

"You prick! I'm not leaving, but I'll try to wrap this thing up. One thing is for sure: you are going to fucking regret making this call by the time I get there."

Leo storms over to Noah's forty minutes after the call. He pounds on the door screaming, "If it's urgent, you should be able to get the door! I don't like waiting!"

As mad as Leo is at his brother, all he can think about is what Mario said to him. *I'm his son, his favorite son at that. Why the fuck is he recruiting from outside*, he kept on thinking.

Noah finally shouts from inside, "The key is under the mat!"

Leo shouts back at him, "That's fascinating. Open the fucking door because I sure as hell ain't doing it!"

"I'm a little preoccupied at the moment."

This fucking prick, Leo thinks. He comes to his senses and lifts the mat, and then he picks up the key. He opens the door and enters.

Leo freezes at the sight of his brother pointing his gun at a seventy percent naked chick. "What the fuck is going on here?"

Noah explains the entire story: a couple of weeks ago, he bought a couple of guns off of an old partner of his father's with whom he had a good relationship with growing up. The guy's name is Pete Abruzzo, and he owns a donut-coffee shop nearby Alfredo's joint. They set a spot to meet where the transaction would take place. Noah attended, but Pete didn't. It wasn't like he was a "no show." He sent somebody else to do it. Noah, who was offended, still bought the guns. The next day, he went to the shop to speak to Pete and wanted to find out why he sent someone else. Pete said he had other things to do that night which was highly offensive to Noah. The next day, Noah stopped by the shop again when Pete wasn't there, put a gun to the worker's head, and stole a dozen donuts. He told the worker to tell Pete that Noah stopped by.

An hour ago, Noah was having some fun with this little Spanish hooker that he currently has a gun pointed at her head. A goon broke in and demanded that Noah would reimburse him for the dozen donuts. Noah paid the total price for the donuts and threw in an extra hundred dollars.

So here is the dilemma: one of the strictest rules of being in a district is that everybody you date, sleep with, or marry has to be somehow involved with one of the districts. This chick that Noah has on his lap has no clue.

"Jesus Christ. I'm going to have to have dinner with Pete just to make up for this shit. All of this over the fact that he didn't attend a meet-up?"

"It's disrespectful," Noah says. "Don't you fucking get it? He's like an uncle to me. It's unprofessional and just insulting that he didn't make the scene."

Leo sighs and says, "Well, it's time to take care of Ms. Hooker."

"Don't do it," the hooker says. "I can be of service to both of you men for a lifetime without any payment in return. What I've seen in this room will surely not be repeated."

"Baby, you have a nice body and a decent face. But, we sadly can't take any risks." Leo says.

Noah hands Leo the gun. Leo gives him an odd look, not knowing what the hell his brother wants him to do with it.

"She's not my hooker," Leo says. "You do it."

Noah's secret is that he genuinely cares for this girl. He knows she's trash, he knows that she is only with him because cash is involved, and he knows she does the same shit with a bunch of other men. But, he still cares a lot for her.

The hooker begs, "Please! I promise I won't say a word!"

"No can do, this is what has to happen," he says. "Noah, do it now!"

Noah turns to his hooker and says, "I know this isn't intimate, but I do care a lot about you."

She says, "If you do care, you'll let me go."

"Then I guess I don't care that much," Noah says as he pulls the trigger on his gun.

Her brains go all over the couch, and Noah begins to cry. Leo sits next to him and puts his hand on his brother's neck. "I know this is sad. I don't know why this is sad for you, but I'm sure there is a valid reason. However, we have bigger problems to deal with."

"What? The couch? We can get Bruno to replace it by tonight and clean this place up." Noah says.

"No, not the couch," Leo corrects. "Dad is looking to recruit from outside of the family."

"What does that mean?"

"It means that our time left in this business is very, very short, and we have to do something about it."

"He only gave us one chance," Noah replies. "What else can we do?"

7

"That's what we need to figure out, and we have to figure it out fast," Leo says. "Our time is limited, and as you and I both know, our father's patience is short."

"Well, he's coming over tomorrow. Perfect opportunity, don't you think?"

Leo laughs at his brother's stupidity. "How the fuck can we discuss anything about the district when your clueless wife is there?"

Even though the golden rule of the districts is to only have intimate relations with women who are somewhat involved with one of the districts, there is one exception: Noah's high school sweetheart.

When Noah was sixteen, before he knew about the districts, he fell in love with Molly, a fellow sophomore. The relationship was always stressful for Raymond. Part of him wanted his son to find happiness, but he worried they'd go the distance which would create many obstacles, which it does to this day. They never would make him end his relationship with Molly, so they made an exception for him.

"We can create a diversion. We'll tell Molly to decorate the tree. And while they do that, we'll go on the balcony and smoke some cigars."

Leo likes that idea. "Ok. How do we get him to give us another chance? That's where I'm concerned."

"I'm concerned about my safety. That could've been my wife on that couch with me. What would we do then? I'm not killing her. I'm not! I need a safer place."

"How about you stop pissing people off? Nobody will go out of their way from Manhattan to Ossining unless you really piss them off." Leo says.

Noah sighs and says, "I'll apologize to Pete tomorrow."

"No, you'll leave that to me. For now, let's get something to eat at Bambino's, we haven't been there in a while." Leo says.

There is a diner that the two brothers were very fond of during their childhood. They both played for a minor league baseball team in their youth, and after every game, Raymond would bring them to the diner for some shakes and burgers.

Leo and Noah, for a couple of years, lived in Manhattan, so they never had time to grab a bite at Bambino's because Ossining is too far out of their way for just a meal. But, now that Raymond has purchased two small houses for his son's, they finally have the chance to return.

"God, it's been ages since we've been here," Leo says. "Do you think the staff will remember us?"

"This place is under new management. Everybody here is fresh. Look around."

Leo spots an old lady with gray hair. "What about her? Remember Mrs. Bambino?"

"Jesus Christ, she's still here," Noah replies. "God, she was here when we were on the baseball team. She hasn't aged a bit."

"That's because she hit her aging maximum back in fifty-eight. She can't get any more wrinkles, no space left on her face."

Regina Bambino is a lady with high hopes, even though she is working a dead-end job. After her husband passed in the Second World War, she didn't have a lot to do. Seeing Leo and Noah grow up in her diner is all she had to do, and she was okay with that.

Mrs. Bambino goes to the table and is thrilled to see the faces of her boys. "Lord, it's been many, many years since I've seen you."

Leo and Noah hug her, and they kiss her on the cheek. Their mother was never the sweetest when she was alive. She was a lovely lady and a good mother, but she was never sweet. Mrs. Bambino was like their version of a sweet mother. She'd ask how the baseball games would go and would engage in their lives.

"I haven't seen you guys in so long; what's been the hold-up?" Mrs. Bambino innocently asks.

"Mrs. Bambino, it's been only a month," Leo says. "Our mother passed, sadly."

"I'm so sorry," Mrs. Bambino sympathizes. "I don't even know what to say."

"Let's not make anything of it if you don't mind. Could I trouble you for that chocolate milkshake I used to guzzle down when I was in smaller shoes?"

The guy at the table next to theirs gets up and leaves. Mrs. Bambino looks over at the table and sees no cash on the check. "Looks like that fella forgot to tip." Mrs. Bambino says with a sigh.

Leo gives Noah a look. *Those fucking pricks didn't tip this sweet lady,* Leo thinks to himself.

"I'm going to go get some fresh air. I'll be right back." Leo says.

Leo catches up to the prick who didn't tip and asks him, "Did somebody forget to tip Mrs. Bambino?"

Leo gives the guy's gut a nice pounding. He is cautious about hitting the face and tries his hardest to avoid it. "You are going to go back in there and tell her you forgot to tip. I want you to give her a quarter of the entire cost of the meal. Fair is fucking fair. Do you understand?"

After a few more minutes of getting beaten, the guy returns to the diner and gives her a good tip. Leo waits a couple of minutes after he leaves and then comes back inside the restaurant.

Leo sits back at his table and sees his chocolate milkshake waiting for him on the table. "Ah, would you look at that? My milkshake."

"You know what I find interesting? The fact that the minute you go outside for some air is the same minute that guy comes back for the tip," Noah says. "What happened?"

"Would you relax? Nothing happened," Leo assures his brother. "But, I can guarantee you that he will never forget to tip again."

CHAPTER 2:

'TWAS THE NIGHT
BEFORE CHRISTMAS...

*Growing up, Leo and Noah's dad was never the nicest.
That never changed.*

On Christmas Eve morning, Noah is resting happily in his bed and dreams about Naples, Florida. His biggest dream is to retire on the beach in Naples with his wife and his unborn son. Raymond and Sofia would take the two boys every summer, and Noah would fall in love with the warm water and the feeling of hot sand on his back. He loves the idea almost more than he loves his wife.

While Noah and that Spanish hooker were on the couch, Molly was visiting her family in Philadelphia. Her parents were never fond of traveling to New York, and Noah was never fond of her parents. Molly would see them alone, which would always make her upset because she felt like her husband was selfish, which he is deep down.

Molly, returning home at 2:18 AM, climbs into bed with her husband. Noah wakes up and sees his pregnant wife next to him. "Hey, honey," Noah says. "How was Philly?"

"Snowy, but lots of fun," Molly replies. "I got to be an aunt for the first time."

"Honey, you have been an aunt since September."

"Yes, but I never got to hold him. You're not an aunt until you hold your nephew. You're not a dad until you play catch with your son. You're not a mom until you hold your baby for the first time."

"I'll be a dad the second I hold my baby. I don't need to play catch. My pops never played catch with me."

Molly sighs and says, "That's because your dad is an ass."

Noah sits up and aggressively replies, "Hey, my dad is a good man. He provided for me my entire life. Don't you remember who bought us this house?"

He knows it's true that his father is a prick, especially when it comes to Noah. But, Noah still respects his father very much. He always thinks that his father is some kind of genius. It doesn't necessarily bother him that his father favors Leo, but it bothers Molly.

"Honey, you have to stop pretending like you have a good relationship with your father," Molly says. "You are too good of a person. Sure, he bought us a house and left you his restaurant. But, there's more to love than just property."

"Well, now I'm not even sure if I'm getting the restaurant. Neither is Leo. He wants to hire somebody else outside of the family."

When it came to Molly, the district was the restaurant. It wasn't just good for money laundering; it was good for lying to his wife about where he spends ten hours of his weekdays.

"This is what I'm talking about, Noah," Molly says.

"Let's go to bed." Noah insists.

Later in Alfredo's Pizza Party Cafe, Leo and Mario sit at a table with two pizza plates. The store is closed.

"Mario, can I ask you a question?" Leo asks.

"I don't see why not," Mario replies. "What's up?"

"Well, I don't know how long I'll be in this business. It might be a couple of days, or it might be a couple of decades. But, no matter what happens, I'll still be involved with this business even if I'm not working for it. That means I'll have to marry within the districts. Got any single chicks?"

Mario laughs and puts his hand on Leo's. "My friend, I have just the girl for you. Her name is Maria, she's my niece. She owns a downtown restaurant."

"Is that her alias?" Leo asks

"No, she's a legit chef," Mario answers. "She went to a culinary school and can cook some nice pasta. If you go there, ask for the secret sauce on your Rigatoni. It's to die for."

"She's not in the business?"

"Every family member is "in" the business, just not all of them work for it. Kind of like your situation."

"Hey, I'm working in this business," Leo says. "Noah and I made a mistake. We sent Abruzzo's guns to the wrong address. But, I'm going to work my fucking ass off to stay on top."

"Well, my dad and your dad have been best friends for a long, long time. If I've learned anything from your dad, it's that he gets what he wants. And right now, he wants you and your brother out and somebody else in."

Leo nods and says, "I should go. I have to meet with Abruzzo. And then I'm going to go to dinner at Noah's tonight."

"Your old man is gonna be there?"

"With some skank that he picked up from somewhere in Brooklyn."

"Then that's your opportunity."

Leo has to meet with Mr. Abruzzo to make up for what happened with Noah. The Abruzzo District and the Santino District don't have a partnership. However, it's always wise to maintain a good relationship with every district so that you don't have to worry about any hits.

Leo doesn't bother calling or giving Abruzzo any notice because he knows that he will close up shop and avoid him at all costs. When Leo enters, he sees Pete talking to one of his employees behind the counter.

The employee says, "We are at a shortage with the Bear Claws, Apple Fritters, and the double chocolate donuts."

"What's wrong with the double chocolate donuts? I just saw a bucket of chocolate spread." Abruzzo asks.

"We're out of chocolate sprinkles."

"We have a shipment coming in. If they ask for the Bear Claws or Apple Fritters, just make some shit up." Abruzzo says.

When Abruzzo notices Leo standing in front of the counter, he doesn't know what to do. "Could I get some Bear Claws and Apple Fritters?" Leo asks.

"We're at a shortage, so why don't you just rob them like your scummy brother," Abruzzo says. "Jerry, why don't you go in the back for a moment."

Jerry goes to the back of the store. "Look, I'm not looking for trouble. I'm looking for peace."

"Fuck peace. Your brother got justice; that's all I'm going to spare for you two." Pete insists.

"Look, my brother is a fuck up. Do you think that I'm not aware of that? I want to give you some money, that's all."

"I already got reimbursed for the dozen. I don't want another nickel from any of you. Get out."

Leo takes out his wallet and takes out twenty bucks. "You had to pay that goon to attack my brother. That costs money. How much did you pay him?"

"I didn't pay him anything. He owed me a favor." Pete explained.

"Then let me do you a favor. Anything. I don't like bad blood, and I sure as hell don't want it."

Pete smiles and says, "Fine. You owe me a favor. When I think of one, I'll give you a holler."

Leo shakes Pete's hand and moves on with his day, and that's how it goes. Nothing lasts long when it comes to bad blood.

Molly isn't the sharpest tool in the shed, but she can whip up a fantastic meal. She bakes her famous Sourdough bread as an appetizer for Christmas Eve before the excellent strip steak she makes.

While she cooks, Noah reads the paper in the kitchen. He loves the smell of her cooking. When it comes to her pasta, she'd give Noah taste tests to see if the noodles are thawed enough for his liking.

Molly and Sofia used to be two peas in a pod. Every time there was a family dinner, the two would go on and on about things the guys didn't care to hear about most of the time. That's when the guys would go on the balcony and smoke Cubans, which they'd only smoke on Christmas Eve due to the rarity.

"It's going to feel odd not to decorate the tree with your mother," Molly says.

"Definitely," Noah replies without actual regard.

"While you guys are smoking your cigars, who's going to decorate the tree with me?"

"The chick that he's bringing over," Noah says. "He picked her up in Brooklyn."

"It won't be the same. Your mother had such a friendly and welcoming way about her. She was almost like a mother to me."

"She was almost like a mother to me, too." Noah says.

"What does that mean?" Molly asks.

Noah doesn't care enough to get into it. The unique smell of the sourdough is slowly fading, and Noah's reading the last article.

"I'm going to take a bath," Noah says. "If you'd care to join me, you're more than welcome to."

"Noah, don't walk away from my question," Molly says. "What do you mean by almost?"

"I mean what you think I mean," Noah snaps. "I love my mother. But, when she passed, she asked Leo to hold her hand. She had her right hand free and didn't say a word to me. Ever since, I've held some resentment, can you blame me?"

"Yes, I can. Your dad plays the same shit on you, and you never complain."

"My dad is a brilliant man. If he favors Leo, he probably has a reason. And don't you get in the middle of my emotions. My father is a great man; my mother was a good woman. That's all there is to it, ok? Now I'm going to take a bath. If you'd like to join me, you're more than welcome to."

Noah always makes sure that his temperature is just right. Whenever he gets mad, he makes it cold so it can relieve his stress. Today, he makes the water colder than Antarctica.

Sometimes, he'll lower his head into the water and soak in that feeling of discomfort because of the cold. He'll open his eyes, and he'll see him and Leo swimming in a pool. Every now and then, his imagination takes a turn for the worst, and this imaginary pool that he's lying on the bottom of starts to turn as red as blood. After he sees his pool turn into blood, he'll stick his head out of the water.

He'll express this vision of his to Leo. He always wonders what the blood was for or who's blood it was. Leo kids and says, "It's because you're on your period, you fucking chick. Relax."

But deep down, Noah knows that this vision is more than just his imagination. He wants to tell Molly or a psychiatrist, but he knows he'd have to say the whole story to get real help.

Noah started having this vision when he turned twenty-eight, nearing the time when he took over the business.

In the late afternoon, somebody knocks on Noah's door. When Noah answers, he sees his dad with his arm around a chick that's young enough to be on a Playboy. *There must be a forty-year difference between the two,* Noah thinks. However, Noah keeps these thoughts to himself and lets his dad and his tramp enter his home.

Her name is Lola. She is blonde and dumb, which is all Raymond needs to know. She used to be a model, but then thought her life was worth more than just exploiting herself.

Raymond sits on the couch as Noah fixes him up a Conya, his dad's signature drink. The two watch TV as they drink.

"Where's Leo?" Raymond asks.

"Leo's on his way," Noah says. "He gave me a ring before he left. Said he'll be here in about twenty minutes."

"Twenty minutes from the time he made the call or twenty minutes from now?"

"Twenty minutes since he made the call. So, it shouldn't be much longer."

Raymond, pretending that he's not replacing him, asks, "How did that make-up meeting go?"

"I couldn't tell ya," Noah replies. "I didn't go. I was busy."

"Busy? Busy doing what? You had a big meeting; what could've possibly been more important?"

Noah looks over to his dad on the other side of the couch and pictures his hooker's dead body. While Noah and Leo went out for a bite at the diner, they had Bruno's guys clean up and replace the couch.

"What does that have to do with anything? I missed a meeting. Big fucking deal."

"You're right, Noah. It is a big fucking deal. This make-up meeting was your chance to apologize to the heads."

"I don't have time to beg for forgiveness," Noah claims. "We made a wrong delivery. I understand and accept that I made a mistake. That's it. If they don't want to accept that, there's not much more I can do."

"Yes, but when you attend these meetings, it shows you care," Raymond explains. "Eventually, Noah, the flock is gonna migrate without you."

Noah doesn't even know what that means. Raymond isn't the best father, friend, or husband, but he is undeniably wise.

"Pops, I don't want you to worry about anything anymore. Why can't you just retire?" Noah says all of this and tries his best to avoid any talk of replacement.

"I'm not going to let you take over if you aren't ready." Raymond insists as he drinks. Before Noah can respond, Leo knocks on the door.

At the dinner table, Raymond sits beside Lola as he tells the story of how they met, "So, I was at this steakhouse with an old friend of mine. We are having a grand old time until our waitress spills water on my lap. So, I'm wet, and I'm furious. I'm yelling and hollering at her. She takes me in the back, and the next thing you know, we have one of the best nights ever. How about that?"

"Great story, pops," Leo says. "I'm sure that that's what God had in mind for us to talk about at the dinner table on Christmas Eve."

The entire table laughs. Raymond asks Lola, "Did I not tell you he was funny? He's a fucking comic."

"A comic is a stretch. Groucho Marx is a comic, and I'm just a funny man with hair like Sinatra's."

During that dinner, the family tells many stories. Noah talks about his love of Florida, Molly talks about the pregnancy, Raymond talks about Lola, Lola talks about fashion.

"I'm so sad that she's leaving us and going back to Italy." Raymond says as he kisses her hand.

"Oh, I'll come back to visit. It'll be ok."

"Hey, I got a story for you guys," Leo says as he looks at Noah and then at his father. "There's this guy at work, right? His name is Patrick. Patrick was originally going to take over his father's restaurant. His father let him have a go at it, and he made one mistake. Only one."

Raymond sees where this is going as Leo goes on with his made-up story. He gives Leo a cautionary look as if he's trying to warn him.

"This is a family restaurant. It has been this way for generations. So, Patrick's father hires from outside of the family. Completely going against everything the business stands for."

Noah says to Molly, "Honey, why don't you take Lola downstairs to decorate the tree? Us men will puff on some cigars on the balcony."

"I no longer puff," Raymond says. "I'm getting older, and my lungs are getting weaker."

"Then pops, you can enjoy a drink while we enjoy a Cuban." Noah suggests.

On the balcony, Noah takes out his box of Cuban cigars. Raymond is furious with Leo.

"What the fuck was all of that about?" Raymond screams.

"Pops, you know what the fuck that was all about," Leo replies. "You're seriously hiring from the outside?"

"Can you blame me? You sent guns to the Jersey clients, not the Chicago clients. We lost both of them, and that took down a lot of our business."

"That's a fucking great story. Guess what? I've heard it a million fucking times. We need to move on from this. Give us another shot."

"Another shot? To do what? Make me lose another client? I'm going to have to pass on that one." Raymond says as he takes a cigar from the box.

"I thought you didn't puff anymore," Leo says.

"I was fucking lying," Raymond replies. "Now, look, I care about you two dearly."

"Not enough. After all of the shit I've done for you, how could you do this to us? Or even to me?" Leo asks.

"All you've done for me? Are you serious? All you ever did was kiss my ass so you could take it all."

Noah, deep down, is relieved to hear his dad call Leo out. He never expresses his feelings to his father, but he smiled when his dad said what he said.

"How the fuck was I a kiss ass? I didn't know you ran a district or even what the fuck a district was!" Leo screams.

"No, but you knew there was something. You knew I had a nice house, nice car, and you knew that there was some money behind me."

Leo doesn't respond to that because he knows that it's true. He always felt like if his father truly loved him more than Noah, which he did, then he'd take everything home with him.

"Guys, I've done a lot for you. I bought you both houses. I got you both cars, and then Noah crashed his. You'll get all of my money when I pass. How bad would it be if you didn't run the district?"

"It's not about the money; it's about the legacy. I thought you'd know that by now." Leo says.

"I'll give you one more shot," Raymond says. "But, I don't want to hear another word from you guys if it goes south. Agreed?"

They both nod to the deal. Raymond takes the lighter and lights his cigar, and then starts telling a story, "When I was just a kid, I had a good friend. A best friend. His name was Richie. He and I were close pals for a very long time. After I came back from the war, your grandfather passed the district down to me. Richie had no idea what the fuck a district was, but he knew I had money. He asked for a loan of two thousand dollars, which was quite a hefty amount of money twenty-seven years ago. He said he needed to start his pizza business and that he'd double what I gave him. So what happens?"

Leo sarcastically says, "I have no clue, but I'm on the edge of my fucking seat."

"He dips. Never saw that man again. A couple of weeks ago, an old friend of mine who knew Richie took his family to Chicago. And my friend is long retired. Guess what he sees? A pizza shop ran by Richie. Richie's Pizza Palace. He couldn't kill Richie; he was with his family. But I know where he is now. You two are going to go down there and get my money back."

"Oh, that's too easy. I bet Richie will give us the two thousand right when I tell him we're your sons."

"Two thousand? No. That was twenty-seven years ago. I want ten." Raymond says as he lets out a puff.

"Ten thousand dollars is a substantial amount of money," Noah says. "Perhaps, we should take what you originally gave him. We are supposed to play fair, aren't we?"

"I see what he's saying," Leo says. "The two thousand he gave him back then is around the ten thousand he wants right now. Remember, this was decades ago."

"So, do we have a deal?" Raymond asks.

Noah takes out his hand and gives his father a respectful handshake. "Noah, go inside. I need a quick word with your brother."

After Noah leaves, Leo asks, "What's wrong?"

Raymond slaps Leo in the face so hard that it hurts his own hand. Leo puts his hand on his face and cries, "What the hell was that for?"

"If you ever put me on the spot like that in front of Noah's oblivious wife, or any oblivious person for that matter, I will grab you by your collar and belt and throw you off of this fucking balcony. You're a big boy now. It's time to put your big boy pants on. I have no time for this anymore."

'Twas the night before Christmas and all through the house,
Leo didn't speak a word to anyone, not even Molly's spouse,
With those Cubans, the boys ruined their lungs,
Smoke was puffed, carols were sung,
As the night grew and grew, Leo's fear got stronger and stronger,
Fear that he's Raymond's favorite no longer.

CHAPTER 3:

BUSINESS TRIP

Any district is all about fairness.

The only thing that Noah can think about all Christmas morning is how he's going to tell Molly that he is going to Chicago with Leo. Usually, he wouldn't be so nervous. But, since they have to drive instead of fly, Noah can't think of the proper explanation. You have to go by wheels for any business trip because you can't smuggle guns past security.

For a long time, it wasn't like that. But, in 1972, three hijackers tried to fly some planes into a nuclear reactor. By January 5th of 1973, the Federal Aviation Administration made it mandatory to check luggage from all passengers, which completely screwed the districts over.

Noah guzzles down hot cocoa after hot cocoa as he tries to think of the right words. After much contemplation, he thinks of an excuse.

"Leo and I have a buddy down in Chicago," Noah says, with Leo by his side. "He's about to get married, and he invited us to his wedding."

Molly giggles and replies, "Kind of last minute, don't you think?"

"Well, this friend of ours… he's a last-minute kind of guy," Leo explains. "It's not going to be a big ceremony. Just close friends, that's all."

"What is this friend's name?"

"His name is Rocco," Noah answers. "Moved to Chicago about five years ago. Nice guy."

"I'm surprised that I haven't ever heard of him, you guys sound very close, and I've been with you for half of your life," Molly says. "I'll go with you."

"What? No. Sorry. I can't bring you. It's only for close friends, remember?"

"Yeah, but you can still bring your wife," Molly says. "I'm sure he'd love to meet your wife."

"He would love to meet my wife. He just wouldn't love to meet my pregnant wife."

"What do you mean by that?"

"Rocco's fiancé is infertile. They tried to have a baby, but they just couldn't. It would break their hearts to see you all knocked up and beautiful. Do you see what I'm getting at?"

She nods and says, "Normally, you wait until after you're married to try for a kid."

"They aren't as traditional as we are," Noah says.

"Ok, then why go by car?"

"Why not? A little brother bonding never hurt anybody." Leo answers.

"But, you two see each other every day at the restaurant. Just fly by plane or go by train; it's safer and faster."

"Honey, don't you worry about our safety. After Leo and I graduated from high school, we took a road trip down to Connecticut to see The Beatles. Remember how you were so worried?"

"Yes, I remember the Beatles trip. I'm still offended that you didn't take me."

Noah hugs her and says, "Honey, I'll make a stop every hour on the hour to give you a ring from a payphone. Ok?"

"I also want pictures from the wedding," Molly says.

Once they exit the borough, Leo starts to take a nap. "Are you fucking kidding me? You're going to leave me alone with nobody to talk to?" Noah barks.

"Hey, this is your shift," Leo says. "What you care to do when it's my shift is up to you. I'm not too fucking thrilled about this trip. So if I want to take a fucking nap, a fucking nap is what I shall take."

Leo takes out a mask to cover up his eyes as he reclines his chair down. Then, Noah takes a cola can out of a little bag in the backseat while keeping his eyes on the road as much as he can. Noah takes a cigar out of the cigar box and lights it up. He pops it open and then turns on the radio. The radio distracts Leo from his slumber.

"Could you turn that shit off? I'm trying to get some shut-eye." Leo says.

"You're not even talking to me," Noah replies. "If I don't have something to do, I'm going to lose my fucking mind."

"What do you want, a ball of yarn? Want me to get a laser pointer and move it around the dashboard as you try to catch it? Want me to give you a bone to chew? Would that keep you content?"

"Fine. I'll just puff cigars and drink soda for the next five hours. Oh, for the love of God. Why the fuck aren't we taking a train? Let's just take a fucking train to Chicago." Noah shouts.

"You know how pops has a strict policy about not going on trains."

Raymond prohibits the boys from giving a single nickel to any train ever since Henry got caught carrying unconcealed weapons. That was the start of the feds keeping their eyes on Henry, which ultimately led them to keep their eyes on everybody.

"Fuck pops! He treats you like shit, and now he treats me like shit. He slapped me on Christmas Eve. Said he didn't have any time for favorites anymore." Leo rants.

"Oh, poor Leo. He isn't favored anymore. Welcome to the last thirty years of my life."

"Fuck it, I can't sleep," Leo says. "You have me all ramped up now."

Leo reaches for a cigar, but then Noah slaps his hand. "I don't like it when you smoke angrily. You get too crazy."

"Smoking is meant for times of anger. What the fuck else am I supposed to do?"

"Relax. Maybe we should just pull over at a gas station and get some air." Noah suggests.

"Just keep driving. I want to get there as soon as possible, and I want to get back as soon as possible."

"We have other problems," Noah says. "Molly wants pictures from the wedding. What the fuck are we going to do?"

Leo laughs and says, "This is why we marry from inside of the districts."

"If you use that shit against me again, my fucking head is going to explode."

"I can't have that happen," Leo says. "The blood will stain my suit."

The two brothers laugh and go back to being buds again. That's how it would always go. They'd fight, and then one of them would crack a joke and ultimately kill the intensity.

"So, how's the baby doing? Have any names in mind?" Leo asks.

"Sure. For a boy, we're doing Adam. For a girl, we are doing Isabel."

"Adam isn't Italian. Are you not going to continue the legacy?"

"Adam is Molly's brother. We're naming the baby after the brother." Noah explains.

"I'm your brother, and my name is Leonardo. Why not Leonardo? It's Italian." Leo complains.

"I don't call the shots with the baby. She's the one who has been carrying it for nine months."

"So? You're the one who is covering the payments for the next fifty years."

"I can't agree with you more," Noah says. "To tell you the truth, it's been a rocky road for us lately. If there is anything I can do to make her happy, I will do it."

"What if she wants to go to a nudist party? Would you do it?" Leo asks.

"I guess I would. It depends on whose party it is. If it's Steve McQueen's party, I'll have to pass. She'd keep her eyes under the belt the whole time."

The two laugh again and continue to crack more jokes.

A couple of hours later, Leo starts to feel the need to go and take a leak. Noah takes this as a chance to give Molly a call. Molly is never too good at long-distance separation. She fears he would sleep with other women.

Noah dials in his home number and says, "Hey!"

From the other side of the phone, Molly responds, "Hey. How is the trip so far?"

"Well, I'm beat to shit. We just stopped to get gas, and Leo is taking a piss. It's his shift now."

"Take a nap. You sound exhausted. And you don't have to feel obligated to call every hour if it's an inconvenience."

"Speaking with the love of my life is never an inconvenience," Noah says. "How is Adam or Isabel?"

"He or she is good, not too much kicking lately. I've just been cleaning up around the house."

"That's good. I'm going to have to leave you now, but I love you."

"Love you."

They enter Chicago at around midnight. Leo has to wake up Noah from his nap because they forgot a major component of the trip: where to stay.

"Just pull over at a motel," Noah says. "We'll only be here for one night."

"In Chicago? A motel in Chicago? Do you know what's in Chicago? Crime. Death. Murder. Unsafe motels. Do you want somebody to break into our room?"

"Would you rather camp out in this car? We don't have that many options."

"Relax," Leo insists. "We can just crash at a hotel like normal fucking people. Hotels are much safer."

In their hotel room, with only one bed because it's a late booking, Leo is drawing a circle around where Richie's pizza joint is on a map of the city. "This is where it is. It's about a twenty-mile drive from this place. I want to be in and out." Leo says.

"Did pops say anything about whether we can kill him or not?" Noah asks.

"Like always, we only kill if it comes down to his life or ours. This is one of his old best friends. We can't do that to him. Or we can, but we just can't tell him."

Richie's Pizza Palace serves deep-dish pizza, which is almost the only thing that people order in Chicago. It's one of the most popular joints in Chicago; something about the crust makes people go crazy.

The line is long, like usual. "So, tell me about this deep-dish pizza," Noah says.

"They put the sauce on top of the cheese. It doesn't make much sense, but it tastes pretty good."

"When the fuck did you get the chance to try it?" Noah asks.

"Pops took me to Chicago when I was fifteen," Leo says. "Don't you remember when we were gone?"

"I try not to remember most of my youth," Noah replies. "I do vaguely recollect a business trip pops took you on. I just don't remember where."

Leo and Noah are next in line. An employee says, "Welcome to Richie's Pizza Palace; what can I get for you?"

"Uh, one slice of deep-dish pizza. Or is it a slice? What the fuck am I calling these things?"

"No worries, sir. I know what you mean. And for your friend?"

"Yeah, I'll get the same thing that he's getting. But, can you bring out the manager for me?"

The employee asks, "Is there something wrong?"

"Nothing three grown men can't handle," Leo insists. "Just send him to that table right over there. And how much will the pizza slices be?"

"Two dollars."

"Expensive pies, huh?" Leo says as he hands her the money.

They walk to the table they pointed to earlier and sit down. "Let's be straightforward. No funny business. We take the ten and then dash." Leo says.

"C'mon, I wanna have a little fun with this," Noah says. "He fucked over pops. This calls for a bit of revenge."

"Would you stop with the whole "pops" thing? He is just as big as a crook as this Richie character. Why the fuck do you care about what the fuck happens to pops? All he does is use you for loyalty."

"I don't know what the fuck you're talking about," Noah snaps. "For the past thirty years, you've been kissing his rear eight days a week. And now he slaps you? Now he says you are not his favorite? Maybe you're a prick about pops because you know that if you're not the favorite, then I have to be."

"He didn't say I wasn't his favorite. He said he didn't have time for favorites. That goes for you too, buster. Would you just forget about it?" Leo rants.

Noah sighs and says, "God forbid, Noah has some attention from time to time."

"Is that what all of this soap opera shit is about?"

Richie approaches the table. He wears a blue buttoned shirt and black pants. He is old but doesn't look very old.

"Heard that you two gentlemen wanted to have a word with me," Richie says.

"Take a seat. My name is Leo, and this is my brother, Noah." Leo says as they give each other a nice firm handshake.

"Nice to meet you two. Is there something that I can do for you two?"

"Actually, there is. Do you have time to take a little jog down memory lane?" Leo asks.

"I'm sorry, I don't think I get what you mean."

Leo smiles and says, "You will in just a skinny minute. This is a nice little pizza shop you've got yourself here, huh?"

"Yeah, it's pretty good," Richie says. "What about it?"

"How long have you had it? Was it passed down to you? Did you marry into it? Did you build it from the ground up?"

"I've had it for around forty years. And I built it from the ground up." Richie says.

Leo is slowly reeling in this fish, and he's enjoying every single second of the process. "Boy, forty years. It must've cost you quite a couple of bucks back then to build a place like this. How did you afford it?"

Richie gets a little nervous as he replies, "I took a loan."

"From who or what? The bank? A friend? Your dad?"

"From a friend of mine. I'm sorry, what does this have to do with anything?"

"You look like a stand-up guy," Leo says. "I'm sure you reimbursed your friend. Right?"

Richie gulps and says, "Why, of course. I even gave him double what he gave me."

Leo smiles and says, "I learned something today. Willis Tower is apparently the tallest building in the states. And you know what else I learned? The owner of Richie's Pizza Palace is a fucking liar!"

Leo takes out a photograph of a younger Raymond next to a younger Richie. Richie tears up as he says, "I think I have to return to my office."

Leo takes out his gun and pushes the tip onto Richie's pelvis. Leo says, "I think you have to stay where you are."

Noah, remaining silent, gets worried. "Leo, put your gun away. There are people in this restaurant."

"Yes, listen to your friend," Richie says.

"He ain't my bud; he's my brother. We're twins. Twins of a man named Raymond Santino to whom you owe a lot of money. Now, you have two options. You can be compliant and give us the money, and we'll go about our day. Or, you can be uncooperative, and I'll blow your fucking balls off with my pistol. Then, I'll go in the back and take the money. Either way, we get the money. Be smart. If the next words out of your mouth aren't about the money, you can say goodbye to your members under the belt."

Richie, who is now sobbing, says, "Fine. Do you want the money? I'll bring it to you. Four thousand dollars, right?"

"Ten thousand. We're talking about many fucking years ago. You're lucky we aren't taking twenty." Leo says.

"It's in the back. But not all of it is back there. I don't carry ten thousand dollars. I have about four thousand back there. That's all. Just stay here, and I'll bring it over."

"I find it hard to believe that you have the exact amount of what you owed my father forty years ago in the back. We're going with you."

In the backroom, they throw Richie onto the floor, and Leo starts kicking his ribs as he says, "Get the fucking money. We don't have all day, and we don't have all night. Cough it up."

Richie goes to the safe and puts in the code. "This isn't what Raymond would want. I bet he's dead, and you just want the cash for yourself."

"Who the fuck do you think sent us? Give us the fucking money, you scum!" Leo shouts.

"Would you keep your fucking noise down? There are employees and customers out there." Richie says.

"Guess what, pal, I don't give a fuck if Kennedy is reincarnated and standing right outside of those doors," Leo says. "I don't give a flying fuck about what's out there; I only give a fuck about what's in the safe. And soon, if you don't give us our fucking money, you're gonna give a fuck about the bullet I put in your neck."

"He is right," Noah says. "Keep the volume to a minimum. We don't need anybody hearing anything."

"Do you want to keep siding with this prick? Weren't you just saying that you wanted to get revenge for pops?"

Richie finally opens the safe and takes out a bunch of stacks of bills. "Ok, here. Take it."

Noah counts and says, "That's the four thousand he said he had. Guess that he wasn't lying."

"Four thousand? We want ten. We aren't getting out of your hair until we're square."

"Ok, there is another solution," Richie says. "We can just run over to my house and get the rest."

"We don't have time for that," Leo says. "You have a family. We don't need anybody seeing this."

"Nobody will rat. I'll tell them the truth about the situation. If they rat on you, they rat on me."

"Fine. But, you are giving us an extra thousand on top of that ten for the trouble you're putting us through. Make that two." Noah says.

"C'mon Leo, let's just take what is rightfully ours. No more, no less." Leo says.

"Yeah, pal. C'mon. I get that I fucked up by ditching your father, but put this situation from my perspective. When I asked him for that two thousand, it barely made a dent in his bank account. Losing that two thousand meant nothing to him. If you took ten thousand from him today, it still wouldn't affect his money. But, taking ten thousand from me does a lot. That's the money for my grandson's college tuition. So, two thousand on top of that ten is too much."

"That's a really nice story. You should be an author. Until then, I want two thousand on top of that ten. Ok?"

When Leo and Noah get back home, they have the twelve thousand dollars in a small bag and set it on a table in front of Raymond in the private room in Russo Santino. As Raymond counts the money, he starts to look a little puzzled.

"Did we knock it out of the park or what?" Noah asks with enthusiasm.

"Well, I must say that I'm perplexed," Raymond starts. "I'm counting an extra two thousand dollars in this bag. Would you two like to explain to me why I'm counting an extra two thousand dollars?"

"For our trouble," Noah answers. "He felt bad that we had to come all of this way just to fix a mistake he made forty years ago."

"So, you're telling me the same bastard who changed locations just to not pay me back gave you two additional two thousand for your trouble?" Raymond asks.

"What the fuck is this? An interrogation? You have the money. Just give us the additional two." Noah says.

"You fucking stole from him," Raymond says. "I know you did. I know that man very well, and he did not change during these forty years. I just know it."

"Ok. We stole it." Noah says.

"He stole it. I had no part in that aspect." Leo corrects.

"I don't fucking care who stole what from who," Raymond says. "This isn't how we conduct our business. We take whatever is ours, and that's it. When you take more, it gives the other party the right to come back. It starts a war is what it does."

"What? Do you seriously think that we are going to war with a deep-dish pizza man?"

"It still isn't right. That man is important to me. Richie was a good man. He made a bad mistake. He's still a brother to me. You robbed a good man."

"This is none of your concern anymore. We did the job. We take over. That was the deal."

Raymond grabs the bag and says, "Fine. You take over in three weeks. I have to get my affairs in order."

Noah ends up telling Molly that he didn't have the pictures because she left his friend at the altar. As always, she believes the story.

Raymond takes a train down to Chicago with a bag that carries two thousand dollars. He knows that it's only fair to return the money to Richie himself.

When he arrives at the joint, he asks to see Richie. The employee goes to the back and then comes back to report he doesn't feel comfortable.

"Tell him that it's Raymond Santino. I just want to have a quick word with him at one of the tables. Tell him that it'll be worth the two minutes."

Richie eventually comes out from his office, and Raymond gives him the additional two thousand dollars that Leo stole. The two end up talking for hours, and when Raymond left, he knew where he would reside after his retirement.

CHAPTER 4:

BAM!

Baseballs aren't just for baseball.

Robert Bruno is flipping through his mail on a standard Sunday morning. He has a warm cup of coffee by his side. "From Noah Leone. What the hell is he sending mail to me for?"

Noah Leone is a part of the Bruno District staff. He's Robert's right hand man.

Robert opens up the envelope and takes out a wedding invitation.

You Are Invited To The Wedding Of
Noah Leone + Selena Esposito!
Wedding Will Be Held at St. Corleone's Church -
Reception Will Be Held At 806 Barrio Dr.
January 12th, 1979

He laughs and says to himself, "I hate going to these things."

Meanwhile, Leo is in the kitchen in his home watching the news from the living room TV as he pours coffee into his mug. Leo's phone starts to ring, and he says, "Damn it."

He picks up and asks, "Can I help you?"

"Hey Leo, it's Pete Abruzzo," Pete says through the phone. "Did I catch you at a bad time?"

"Pete, Carter is in office," Leo jokes. "It's always a bad time."

Pete laughs and asks, "Can you stop by the shop for just one second, please?"

"Yeah, I'll be right there. Should I invite Noah or not?"

"You're going to need him," Pete says before he hangs up.

Leo owes Pete a favor, and that's one of the worst positions to be in when it comes to the districts. Any head of any district takes advantage of favors. When somebody owes you a favor, you think big. When it comes to favors in the districts, the punishment never fits the crime.

Leo dials in Noah's number and says, "Get your ass over to Abruzzo's shop."

Leo hangs up and then takes one last sip from his coffee.

In the donut shop, Leo is taking down a bunch of glazed donuts. Noah doesn't get to eat anything because it was his fault this whole thing is going on in the first place.

"Now, let's cut right to the chase," Pete says. "There is a man named Noah Leone."

"Ay, my name is Noah, too," Noah says.

"Do you want a fucking medal? Anyway, he works for the Bruno District. I hired him to kill somebody. Long story short, he killed the wrong guy. I need him dead. I don't need to see the body; I don't need it to be clean; I need it to be done. Normally, I could ring up Robert and get one of his guys to do it, but it's one of Bruno's guys that I'm after. It's his cousin."

"Where does this guy live?" Noah asks.

"I wrote it on this slip of paper," Pete says as he hands them the slip. "Do it however you want. However, he has pitbulls. These fuckers are trained to rip your ass apart. So, try to stay out of the downstairs area."

"How else can we do it?" Leo asks.

"There are two windows on the front of the house. His bedroom window is to the right. Make it happen."

They decide to go to Bambino's Diner for some brunch, and they contemplate a plan from there. Leo orders the chicken and waffles, and Noah orders the steak and eggs.

"Ok, how about a long and extensive ladder?" Noah suggests.

"Do you know the length of his house?"

"Of course, because I go over there every single day," Noah says sarcastically. "I don't know the fucking length. I'm sure it's not that big of a house; Bruno's guys' aliases wouldn't cover a ginormous house."

"I don't want to use a ladder," Leo says. "Too risky. We don't want any neighbors spotting two men climbing up a ladder into the house. I don't even want to enter the house."

"How else are we going to get this guy?"

"Remember what pops told us? In this business, you have to get creative. Let's get creative."

"Creative? Pops? I thought you weren't listening to him anymore." Noah says.

"I can say all different types of things about him. However, he's wise. And he's right. We can't get in the house because there are pitbulls that'll rip our members off, so we have to think outside of the box. We'll get him from the outside."

"And how are we going to do that? Give him a call and ask if he can look out of the window?"

Leo's eyes go wide open, and he smiles and says, "Noah, you are a fucking genius. We need to get him to look out of the window!"

"How else would we shoot him? Also, how are we going to get him to look outside of his window?"

"We create a diversion," Leo starts. "What do you do when kids are playing ball in your neighborhood, and then they knock a baseball through your window? You lookout. That's what we'll do, but at night. We'll use that perfect throwing arm of yours to smash a baseball through the window. When he looks out, I put my Winchester to work. I'm great at sniping. Pops used to take me deer hunting, and I'd pop every deer's head off. This man is my deer."

Noah laughs and says, "You were crazy as a child; you are obscene as an adult, too. Why did you even go back to Pete in the first place?"

"Because of your hurt feelings incident. We needed to get on good terms."

"We were on good terms. He wasn't going to strike back at us. He wasn't contemplating anything."

"If he really wasn't planning on striking back at us, he wouldn't have taken me up on my offer."

Noah understands what his brother is getting at and says, "Sometimes, I hate this business. Sometimes, I love it. But most of the time, I fucking fear it."

"Why do you fear it?"

"What do I fear? I fear that mind of yours is going to get you killed one day. I mean, c'mon. Do you understand the severity of this situation? We are hitting a hitman."

"I get it. If we miss the shot, we're fucked."

"If you miss the shot, we're fucked." Noah corrects.

"Oh, so this all is on me? This partnership is all of a sudden reliant on my success in this operation?" Leo rants.

"It is your plan," Noah points out. "We need to get more partnerships. It's fucking ridiculous that we only have one group that can do a hit for us."

"This isn't the fucking mafia, Noah," Leo says. "It's not as easy as that. We have to be loyal, and we can't replace our go-to hitmen just because of this one occasion. These are rare fucking circumstances. Circumstances that will not repeat themselves. And if they do, we won't owe Pete a favor, so it won't be our problem."

"Sometimes, I wish we were in the mafia," Noah says. "It'd be easier, don't you think?"

"We are in our own version of the mafia. The Santino District can be whatever you want it to be. Regardless, we handle this shit the way it's meant to be dealt with, ok? We are a go-for operation baseball snipe unless you can think of something better."

At 11:09 PM, Leo pulls up to the house with a Winchester that he's borrowing from Raymond in the backseat. Noah is in the passenger seat with a bucket of baseballs that he got from a sporting goods store.

"I should've gotten some more baseballs," Noah says. "I can't believe I didn't take that into account."

"How many do you have in there? Thirty?" Leo asks.

"Twenty," Noah replies. "I have twenty tries. What if this guy has one of those expensive windows that don't shatter easily?"

"Then, in that particular case, don't worry about shattering it. If you hit the window hard enough, it'll hopefully make enough noise to get this guy's attention. But those windows probably aren't that durable. Fiberglass is expensive."

Leo puts the car in park and rolls down his window. Noah steps out of the car and brings the bucket closer to the gate around the house, which is relatively smaller than Noah's place.

Leo picks up his sniper rifle and puts it through the window. "Is your throwing arm as good as it once was?"

"We're about to find out," Noah says. "Don't you think that it's odd that a hitman whose alias is a server at Russo Santino can afford a gate to guard a house like this?"

"I found everything about this business odd at first," Leo says as he adjusts the focus. "However, I've learned to accept the fact that nothing is normal in a business like this."

Noah picks up one of the balls and says, "I'm ready when you are."

"Go for it. I've got it pointed at the right window."

Noah swings his arm back and lets one fly up at the window but then ends up hitting the wall.

"Relax. You have nineteen more tries. And after that, we can go to that store and pick up some more. Take your time." Leo says.

Noah takes a deep breath and swings another ball but misses it by just a few feet. "Fucking hell! I had it lined up perfectly."

"Then why didn't it hit?" Leo sarcastically asks.

"I don't need that right now. Just shut your yapper until that glass is shattered."

Leo jokingly says, "I'm sorry to disrupt your slumber, sir."

Inside the bedroom, Noah Leone and his fiancé, Alice, are lying together and snuggling. "You know, when I was a little boy, there was this band that I fucking loved. The Patties! Boy, oh boy, I fucking loved them. One day, I listened carefully to this one song of theirs. It's called Steam. Let me play it." Leone says.

He goes up to his stack of records and pulls out 'Nevermore' by The Patties. "After my dad dodged, I went through a very long period of intense depression. I even contemplated suicide. I heard this song one day, and everything changed for me."

Leone puts the record on the record player and sets it to the right side. He begins to play the song. "It's beautiful," Alice says.

"Isn't it? I always wondered what the meaning behind it was, and then I made up my own meaning. The steam in this song is like my issues with my father."

"That's so sweet," Alice says.

"This should be our wedding song. Come here and dance with me." Leone says with a warm smile.

"Noah, it's late. We should be getting some rest. We are going to see my parents tomorrow."

"Alice, please. Join me on the dance floor. This is going to be our wedding song, I'm telling you."

She gets up and takes Leone's hand. They start to slow dance along to the song. "I love you so much, Alice."

"I love you a great deal, too," Alice says.

The two begin to kiss as they do the little slow dance that they will do at the wedding.

BAM!

A baseball hits and cracks and the window. "Jesus Christ! What the fuck was that?"

Back down at the car, Noah exclaims, "I hit the damn thing! Am I fucking talented or what?"

"You'll be talented when you demolish the glass. Keep going." Leo says.

Leone and Alice are stuck staring at the window. "Who the fuck did that?"

BAM!

A baseball finishes what the other ball started and breaks that window into pieces. "Ok, now what the fuck is all of this? It's those fucking kids!"

Leone goes up to the shattered window and then opens it up. He hollers, "You run now, you skinny punks! The day I catch you is the day you-"

BAM!

A bullet flies straight through Leone's head, and his blood goes all over Alice, who starts to scream. "Baby! No! Baby! Baby! Baby!" Alice cries.

Noah runs right back into the car, and Leo throws the Winchester in the backseat. "Shouldn't we put it in the trunk?" Noah questions.

"We gotta dodge," Leo says. "Did you hear that chick scream? We don't want her to see us."

"Her husband just got blown up. I doubt she's going to peek out the window to see who's there."

"Whatever, man. Do you want to catch a bite at Bambino's?" Leo asks.

"We already went there today. Let's just go to one of those coffee shops. I could go for some breakfast for dinner."

"Fine. I have one in mind." Leo replies.

Leo likes to eat at diners further away from Bambino's because he doesn't want to support the competition. There is one diner a couple of miles away from Leo's house called Rally's.

When Leo and Noah enter the diner, they spot Raymond talking to a young guy around Leo and Noah's age. It's around ten at night, which makes the situation all the more bizarre.

"What the fuck is going on over there?" Noah asks.

"One of two things. Pops is secretly a queer, or he's hiring from the outside." Leo responds.

CHAPTER 5:

BALCONY BLITZ

Prosperity is a torch to be passed down.

A t the diner table, Leo is furious; Noah is unsure. Noah, being the loyal son that he is, wants to believe that it wasn't what it looked like. Leo, being the smart man that he is, knows exactly what's going on.

"What else would he be doing at a diner with an Italian guy around our age at ten at night?" Leo asks.

"Maybe that's like Antonio's cousin and he wants Raymond to be his confirmation sponsor."

"And they are meeting at ten? Wake up and smell the coffee. He's trying to replace us. A few weeks to get his affairs in order? Are you fucking kidding me?"

"Ok, but let's think logically," Noah says. "If he went behind our backs to replace us, he'd have to know we'd find out. What happens to us then? He knows we'll keep fighting for the position. He'd have to kill us."

"There's a lot of uncertainty in this situation, I know that," Leo says. "One thing is for certain, and that is that we are getting to the bottom of this shit tonight."

Noah is absolutely right. Raymond can't replace them without taking drastic measures. Putting a hit on your own children sounds vicious and vile, which it is. However, this business comes before the family to Raymond.

Leo and Noah patiently wait in the car outside of the diner. They play a one on one game of blackjack to kill time.

"This is just proof that I would kick ass as a dealer in Vegas," Noah says. "I swear to God, I'm considering it as a retirement job. I could get a nice condo in Nevada and be a badass dealer."

"I thought you had your heart set on Naples. Also, people are going to fucking hate you." Leo says.

"People already fucking hate me," Noah replies. "At least now I'll be making money from it."

"No, I'm serious," Leo says. "One time when I went to Vegas with pops, this dealer fucking robbed him. He came in with two grand and left with nothing but a complimentary drink. He tracked down that dealer and fucked him up."

"He killed him?"

"No, if he killed him I would've said that he killed him. He just beat the shit out of the guy."

"When the hell did you and pops go to Vegas?" Noah asks, slightly angry.

"When I turned twenty-one," Leo says. "He got so drunk that he almost got hit by a bus. If I wasn't there, and if I was just half as fucked up as he was, he would've died."

Noah doesn't laugh, just sits and sighs. "Everything a-ok? What's wrong, Noah?" Leo asks.

Noah, very calmly, responds, "Just shut the fuck up, and pass me a cigar and a light."

"Noah, what the fuck did I do? I didn't say anything offensive, did I? What the hell is wrong?"

"Leo, everything is fine. Everything is perfect. Nothing to report. Just pass me a cigar."

"Not until you tell me what's wrong," Leo says. "What the hell is the matter with you? You brought up Vegas."

"Leo, just pass me a fucking cigar," Noah says with his temper increasing. "I don't have time for this shit."

"We have all of the time in the world," Leo replies. "What the fuck is wrong? Is it pops?"

"Yes, it's him. It's you. It's the Vegas trip. It's the hunting trip. It's all of the trips. Will you just shut the fuck up about it and give me a fucking cigar?"

Leo spots the man exit the diner and quickly says, "Noah, it's him. He's here."

"My lungs just got saved by the bell." Noah says as the two of them exit the car.

Leo approaches him and says, "Hey pal, fuck you."

Leo punches him in the face and Noah holds his arms back as Leo unleashes his strength against the man's poor body. "Check if he is carrying." Noah says.

"Good thinking." Leo replies.

Leo pats the man down all around his body in search of weapons of any kind. He pulls up the back of the man's suit and takes out a pistol. "Just that?" Noah asks.

"From what I could find. Load him in the trunk." Leo orders.

The two brothers hold him down and continue to punch the life out of him. Leo unlocks the trunk and opens it up. The two push him in and then lock it back down again.

"Where are we going to go?" Noah asks.

"Baseball field parking lot," Leo says. "Let's make it quick. I'm beat to shit and I have a cold pillow waiting for me at home."

On the ride to the parking lot, it is extremely silent in the car. Noah is lighting the cigar he has been craving and Leo just drives quietly. He thinks about how he spent all of those years sucking up to his father only to be replaced. He feels like he wasted an aspect of his youth, which makes him horribly depressed.

Noah just puffs on his cigar without a care in the world. If the car were to ram into a gas tank and blow up, it wouldn't phase him. He has a son that he doesn't necessarily want on the way, and he loves his wife dearly, but they just don't click. She knows he's lying to her, she just doesn't know what he is lying about. Noah knows that she knows, just doesn't care enough to act on anything. He knows she can't divorce him, she's just a housewife. What would she do and where would she go? Philadelphia?

An interesting development occurs to Leo when they approach a red light. *What would he have done to us after he replaced us,* Leo thought to himself. "What do you really think pops would've done to us after this prick came in?"

"Leo, I'm in a state of extreme tranquility. Please do not disturb me at this time."

"Consider this your wake up call," Leo says. "I hope your trip to euphoria was fun while it lasted. Because guess what…after we go through with this, you won't be going back for a long, long time."

"What the hell are you talking about? I was just trying to relax. Just trying to chill out, you know?"

"We're on a mission to possibly take out our own father," Leo says. "Before we do that, there's no time for relaxation. And after we do that, relaxation ceases to exist. Do you understand?"

"I don't want to do this. Maybe I wanted to just live a normal life. No other district is run by a partnership. I never asked to be a co-boss."

"Do you think I asked for this to be a partnership? Do you think I'm happy with this position? I didn't and I'm not. And if you wanna bitch about it, I'll drop you off at your place and you can fly out to Florida for shelter. I hate this situation just as much as you do."

"There's no fucking chance that you hate this more than I do," Noah barks. "No fucking chance."

"Fine, maybe I do or maybe I don't," Leo says. "Regardless, I hate this situation. But, I'm facing the music and doing what's necessary. First thing he does is try to replace us. Step two is trying to clip us. I'm not letting him get to step two, I'm just not."

Once they arrive at the parking lot, Leo yanks out his pistol and gives Noah the keys. "Pop it open."

"Why the fuck do I have to do it?" Noah asks.

"Because I'm the one who holds the gun. Pop the trunk open, I don't have time for this shit." Leo says.

"Oh, you don't have time for this? No! Fuck that. I'm holding the gun and you are opening the trunk."

"Why the fuck does it matter? Just open the fucking trunk." Leo orders.

"No, we are trading places," Noah says. "I'm not opening the goddamn trunk, you are. It's your trunk anyway."

"Why can't you open the trunk? Do you not know how?"

"What if he tries to attack me?" Noah asks.

"That's what the fucking gun is for," Leo shouts. "Fine, I'll open the trunk if you are too big of a fucking pussy to do it yourself. Give me the keys."

"No, fuck you. I'm not a pussy."

"Then open the fucking trunk. We're wasting time with this meaningless dialogue."

Noah shrugs as he complies and he turns the key and unlocks the trunk. Once he opens it, the man quickly tries to get out, but his back is too weak. Leo laughs at the spectacle and says, "Noah, check this out. He's like a fish out of water."

Leo and Noah pick up the man from both sides of his weak and scrawny body and throw him onto the concrete. "Before we move any further, I have to ask what your name is and you have to answer honestly."

"Francis," the man spits out. "My name is Francis. Please, I have money. I have a lot of money, my dad has a lot of money. I don't know who you guys are or what you guys are looking to score, but I can provide whatever you want. Just don't hurt me, that's all I ask."

"Francis, don't you worry," Leo says. "Nobody is going to lay another finger on you as long as you comply with the truth, the whole truth, and nothing but the truth. Understand?"

Francis nods as he continues to do his obnoxious cry. "Why were you at that diner with Raymond Santino? You will not get hurt whether what you tell us is what we want or don't want to hear, as long as it's the truth. And don't even think about pulling any funny business, I am a human lie detector. And if you don't believe me, try me. And if you try me, you'll receive the wrath of myself and the fury of my pistol."

"Raymond Santino is a friend of my uncle, Antonio," Francis says, which makes Leo smirk at Noah. "Raymond needs somebody to take over his restaurant."

Leo, knowing that he's full of shit, puts the gun up to Francis's head. The frantic man shouts, "Ok, district! District! It was his district!"

"Now, we're getting somewhere! He wants you to take over, doesn't he?" Leo asks very aggressively.

"Yes. He does. He said it would work out because my father doesn't have a district." Francis explains.

"Did he mention anything about his two sons, Leo and Noah? Say what he had in mind for them? Or no?" Leo hollers, starting to lose his sense of volume.

"No, he didn't," Francis says. "He didn't even tell me why he needed somebody to take over, really."

Leo, just to make sure that Francis is telling the truth, pushes the gun on his forehead again. "Tell me the truth, Francis! Did he or did he not?"

"No, I swear to God! I swear to God! You have to believe me! I already told you about the district, why wouldn't I tell you about this?" Francis cries hysterically.

Noah looks deep into the crying man's eyes and can just see that Francis is telling the truth. "Leo, he would've told us by now. He's telling the truth."

Leo knows that Francis is telling the truth, he just wants answers so badly that he's willing to go out of his way just to not believe it. "Very well. Francis, I appreciate your cooperation. I apologize that this had to happen this way, but I'm not sorry that this happened. You are a good man, so is your uncle." Leo says.

"Could we give you some money for the trouble? Or some other method of repayment?" Noah offers.

Francis, frantically and immediately, answers, "No. No. That won't be necessary. I'll be fine just taking a cab."

"I'm sorry, I can't let you leave our sight until we seal the deal. We don't want to risk you giving Raymond a call to warn him of what's to come." Leo says.

Noah starts to worry quickly after Leo says that. *This is starting to get real,* Noah thinks. At first, he thought that this was just Leo bluffing. He never believed Leo for a single second. He doesn't want to believe that his own brother would intentionally kill their own father.

"Are you genuinely contemplating this? You seriously are thinking about murdering our father?" Noah asks with deep concern.

"Rather him than us. You were right. He'd have to kill us if he were to replace us, what else could he do to stop us? It's a game of chess."

"Doesn't matter, it's not going to happen anymore," Noah cries. "We prevented this from happening. We don't have to act on anything, let's just have a civil talk."

"A civil talk? There's nothing civil about this business. The fact of the matter isn't that it's not going to happen because we busted him, it's that if we didn't go to that diner, we'd be done for."

"We don't even know what he would've done. I doubt he would've killed us."

"You didn't doubt it in the diner," Leo says. "What other alternative could there be? He replaces us and kicks us out from the job, he knows we're going to fight. He knows we're going to kill. How could he prevent us from doing that besides a hit?"

Noah knows that Leo is most likely correct about Raymond. Leo says, "We should have never taken that extra money from Richie. That's why this is all happening. If we would've brought what was expected, he wouldn't be looking to replace us."

"So it's all my fault? All of this? Are you fucking serious?"

"You fucked up the address on the delivery."

Leo and Noah both are sure that they are in the right. Leo's thought process is that Noah hit the first domino in the domino chain. Noah's thought process is that if Leo didn't tick off Raymond, he wouldn't be looking for any replacements. In hindsight, they were both right and both wrong. But, when it came to their sibling rivalry, there had to be a winner.

"You are the one who fucked that hooker and made me get Bruno's men to clean it up. You are the one who missed the fucking meeting. I always clean up your fucking messes."

"Say whatever the fuck you want, but I never asked for this," Noah snaps. "I never wanted to be in the district, I wanted to be a businessman."

"Well, Mr. Businessman, nothing would delight me more than if you stepped down and let me do it on my own. I'm not stopping you from being a businessman."

"But, I'm involved now. I have money coming in and a son on the way. I need this job, but I sure as hell don't want it. What I'm saying is, this is a fifty-fifty partnership. We don't do anything unless we both agree."

"Then we won't do anything. We won't kill pops, ok? I will." Leo says as he takes out his keys.

Leo shuts the trunk and then goes into his car and locks the doors. Noah tries to open the door as he screams, "Leo! Leo! Don't you dare drive away! Don't you fucking dare, you prick!"

Leo cracks the window just a little bit and says, "I get that you don't want to kill pops. Ok? I get it. But, it's what we have to do, and soon you will realize that."

Leo starts the car and drives off. Noah, not letting go of the situation, runs after him as he starts to shed tears. "Leo! Leo! Get back here!"

Too late! Leo is already on his way to finish the job. "What now?" Francis asks.

"I have to call him, I have to give him a warning," Noah says as he feels around for his wallet. He doesn't have it. "Fuck, I left it in the car. Do you have fifty cents?"

"You took my wallet." Francis replies.

"Ok, it's not a problem. Not a problem at all. Let's just go to a restaurant and use their phones."

"What restaurants? Everything is closed." Francis points out.

"Well, we have to do something. You have to help me." Noah begs.

"I don't really have a say in it, you have a gun."

A lightbulb turned on in Noah's cranium. "I have a gun. I have a fucking gun!" Noah exclaimed.

Noah thought of a plan, a plan that he knew would work. But, he knew he had to act fast. When Leo is determined to go somewhere and do something, the speed limit signs on the streets are just for decoration.

On the sidewalk on that cold New York night, a married couple walk down the sidewalk and giggle. "Mary, I would never ask your father to sleep on the couch. I will be glad to."

Noah approaches the lovely couple and asks, "Do you have fifty cents that I could have?"

The man says, "Scram. Go get a job."

Next thing you know, there is a gun pointed at the man's head. "I'm not gonna rob you dry. I just need fifty cents."

In the living room, Raymond is eating some leftover steak from his dinner while watching *Magnificent Massacres*, which is a show that he used to watch with Noah. Raymond dabs a bit of A1 on the side of the plate and takes a sip of the frozen margarita he concocted. Raymond's phone rings.

"Hello?" Raymond asks after he picks up.

"Pops, it's Noah. Listen, this is going to sound very bad." Noah says.

Before Raymond can even respond, there is a loud knock on the door, with Leo on the other side. "Hold on, Noah. There's somebody at the door."

Noah knows that it's Leo, but he can't say that he's there to kill him. He knows that a statement like that wouldn't be ignored by any feds who may or may not be listening in on the lines. "Pops, don't answer it! It's Leo! He's going to do something very bad!"

"I'll be right back, I need to answer the door." Raymond says and then sets the phone on the table.

Raymond slowly walks up to the door and then opens it up. He sees Leo, who is smiling, with a box in his hand. "Hey pops, I was getting a little lonely in the house and wanted to know if you'd like to puff a couple of cigars on the balcony. I feel like there is unsettled tension between us."

"Unsettled tension? Are you talking about Richie?" Raymond asks.

"I'm talking about Christmas Eve. The balcony incident. I've been having trouble sleeping since so I think we should talk about it. C'mon pops, I have leftover Cubans."

Raymond laughs and says, "No man can turn down a Cuban. C'mon."

For years, Raymond has been known as a sneaky fox. One who could turn the table very quickly and simply. It's why his district has been so successful. Most districts don't make it past the feds for very long. The only thing that made the feds keep an eye on Santino was because of Russo's conviction. But on that night, the fox fell into the hunter's trap. Raymond and Leo go up to the balcony. Leo knows that he left his morality in the car, and Raymond forgets that he left Noah on hold.

Raymond doesn't even think about Francis or the replacement process itself at all, he's just happy that Leo is over. He may have snapped at him, but he couldn't kid himself; Leo will always be his favorite.

Leo takes out two of the cigars and hands Raymond one of them. "You know pops, I heard a story the other day. A father and a son go on a boat. The son asks: papa, I can grant you four wishes, what are they? The father says: well, it gets a little boring out at sea, maybe a magic VCR that can operate on this little boat. So the son grants his wish and then a magic VCR comes on the boat. The son says: you have three more wishes. The father says: well, I'm kind of hungry, so how about a bucket of buttery popcorn. The son makes a bucket of popcorn appear. The son says: two more wishes. The father says: how about a tape of an episode of *Cornfields in Texas*. So the son makes the tape appear and says: one more wish. The father says: well, now that I have everything I need to maintain a happy life, I wish you'd fucking kill yourself."

Raymond is slightly caught off guard from the end of the story. "What kind of a fucking story is that?"

"It's not a story, it's more of an analogy," Leo says. "I grant you all of these wishes for all of these years and you want me fucking dead!"

Leo yanks out his pistol and points it right at Raymond's head. "Son, what the hell has gotten into you? Put the gun down!" Raymond says.

"I know about Francis! I know about the replacement! I know about it all!" Leo shouts.

"Would you keep your voice down, I have neighbors," Raymond demands. "And who the hell is Francis?"

"Don't lie to me, pops," Leo says as he starts to cry. "You would've had us clipped. Don't lie to me. That's what would have happened, right? Please, just don't lie to me. Keep whatever dignity you have left and tell me the truth."

Raymond looks into the gun knowing deep down that he reached the end of the line. Raymond is a man with many dishonorable features, but he is a man with respect. "Yes, you would have been respectfully and gracefully taken out."

"I didn't know there was a graceful way to murder your children," Leo says. "Learn something new everyday, huh? I'll take you out gracefully then. I'll give you some more time to puff that Cuban."

Raymond says, "Suddenly, I don't like Cubans anymore. Look, if you let me live, I'll give you whatever you want. You can take over."

"Pops, you no longer have my trust." Leo says.

He sighs and then runs up to Raymond and grabs him by his belt and the back of his collar. He pushes him a little off the balcony, but then turns him around so he'll land on his back. "You ready?"

"Son, don't do this. Don't let go. You know that you're my favorite!" Raymond exclaims, and he's not lying.

"I thought you didn't have time for favorites anymore, pops." Leo says.

Leo, with no hesitation, let's go and watches his dad plummet. Raymond ends up landing and falling through a glass table next to the pool and dying immediately, a painless process.

From the balcony, Leo looks down at his father's dead body and watches the blood exit his head and spread across the floor. Before he can leave and act like he had nothing to do with the tragedy, he had to set up a realistic narrative for the scene.

Leo goes down to the spot where his dead father lies. He still has the Cuban stuck in between his two fingers. Leo, very carefully, takes the cigar from the two fingers and exits the scene. He goes into the living room and throws the Cuban into the fireplace and watches it burn out. When the ambulance comes, he doesn't want his father to be seen dead with a Cuban. It would draw too much attention to the family.

Leo goes into his father's bedroom and opens up a drawer from his nightstand and takes out a box of Ashton cigars. He returns to the scene of the crime and sticks one of the cigars in between his fingers again.

Leo walks to his father's liquor cabinet and takes out the large bottle of whiskey that his father prefered. He reaches for the glass cabinet and takes out a small glass and starts to pour the whiskey. After he pours a decent amount, he walks back up to the balcony with the bottle and the glass of whiskey. When he gets on the balcony, he sets the bottle of whiskey on the floor. Next, he aligns the glass of whiskey and drops it near Raymond's body. His job is done.

When he turns around, he sees Noah who has his gun aimed in between Leo's eyes. "Noah, you made it. Good for you."

Noah is scared, sad, angry, and shocked. He can't even hold his pistol without shaking. "You motherfucker! You killed him! You killed pops!"

"Very good, Noah. Somebody's starting to catch on." Leo jokes.

"Oh, you think I'm in a funny mood? Do you think I'm here to crack jokes?"

"I know exactly what you're here to do, so spare the both of us the time. If you shoot me, very well. I'll go to hell, as will you eventually. But, you will have to keep in mind that I saved our fucking asses tonight." Leo spiels.

"By killing our fucking father?"

"It's kind of odd if you think about it," Leo laughs. He takes out two of the cigars in the box of Ashtons and offers Noah one of them, but he refuses. Leo lights his cigar and as he does he says, "Let's say you had one of those time machines. Would you really go back in time to stop me from doing this?"

With smoke blowing in his face, Noah replies, "Abso-fucking-lutely I would. I'd do anything."

"Anything? Well, here's an idea. Let's go back in time. You will probably kill me, or do something else to prevent this occurrence. What happens next? I'll tell you…you die. You know that it's true. You are the one who pointed it out at the diner. So, are you feeling tough? Feeling like a big shot? You and I are both aware of the fact that even though you knew the outcome, you wouldn't have killed him. If you can't kill him, what makes you think you can kill me? So Noah, put the fucking gun down and give your brother a hug. Our father died for fuck sakes."

Leo puts out the cigar on the balcony bars and spreads his arms out wide, offering his crying and shivering brother a hug. At that moment, Noah sank into grief. He let his guard down, along with his gun. He shoves the gun back into the back of his belt and goes in to give his brother a hug.

The two brothers stand there and hug for a couple of minutes. They don't say a word. Once they separate, Noah says, "Well, looks like we are the official heads of the Santino District."

Leo smiles at his brother, who is just an innocent little boy in his eyes, and puts his hand on Noah's shoulders and says, "On paper, yes. But, make no mistake…I'm the head of the Santino District. You are just my little puppet, I run the show. All you have to do is sit at the tables and look pretty. Oh, and by the way…if you ever put a loaded gun to my head again, you won't look that pretty anymore."

On that night in Manhattan at 12:47 AM on Raymond Santino's balcony, Noah witnessed the most terrifying sight ever imaginable…he saw the torch pass down to Leo. A new era has arrived.

CHAPTER 6:

WHITE STUFF

Monkey See, Monkey Do.

Cocaine is a stimulant drug, illegally used for euphoria purposes. It is made from two things: Erythroxylum coca and Erythroxylum novogranatense.

In 1914, The Harrison Narcotics Act was implemented. This act prohibited any sales of coca products in the state of New York.

Cocaine gives you a state of false authority and power. However, the stimulant drug can have health impacting side effects: panic attacks, constant irritation, and nasal damage...in other words, nose bleeds.

After the funeral, Leo gets hit by something he never really considered: what does he do now? Obviously, he knows what he wants to do... he just doesn't know how and neither does Noah.

Noah, who came to terms with the fact that Leo did the right thing that one night, is starting to get in the groove of a district head. He goes out and buys himself some gray suits and black ties. He goes back to Pete Abruzzo, a risky move, and buys himself a few new handguns.

One night at Bambino's, Noah suggests to Leo, "Maybe we should consider going into business with Abruzzo."

The reason why none of the districts have a partnership with Abruzzo is essentially because Abruzzo isn't necessarily a "district". Pete's gig shares the primary function of a district, but he doesn't have any partnerships. Bruno always gets supplies from Abruzzo, but they don't have an official collaboration, and they don't correlate on a day-to-day basis. Why does Pete not have any partnerships? It's pretty simple.

When districts have a group partnership, like how they do, they don't hire from outside of the group.

HYPOTHETICAL SITUATION:

Let's say that Pete is in the group and wants to sell guns to someone outside of the partnership…it can't happen. If he wants to distribute guns, he would have to go through the Santino District for distribution purposes, which would mean Santino gets a cut of the transaction.

Pete wants to make as much as possible, which is why he is a lone wolf. Raymond and all of the other heads have tried to get in business with him many times because there's no other guy in Manhattan who has a variety of guns like Pete. He will never settle.

"Noah, he is a loner. Pops and Bruno have tried to get into business with him for many, many years." Leo explains as he digs into his extra thick chocolate milkshake.

"Well, when we get into business with the clients, some are going to want guns," Noah says. "It would save some money if we had a partnership with him."

"Don't you think that I know that? We have at least two clients that order guns, but they don't need orders that often. There's a fine line between ordering guns and narcotics. Drugs don't last forever. And when you sell them to the crackheads we sell them to, they don't last very long. I'll get the client files from Mario and see how long it's been since the last drug deal." Leo explains.

"Don't you find it insane that we don't have a district that supplies firearms in the group?"

"I find it insane that you don't understand how this works," Leo says. "Pete will never go into business with us, and I don't blame him. He'd be making less; why would he?"

"Well, we can't afford his prices."

"We don't have to, at least not right now. We don't need any more guns."

"Right now, we don't. But, we have to sell these things whether they ask for them or not."

Leo laughs and says, "Why would we try so hard to sell guns that we don't have?"

"Because it'll generate money. The clients don't want any new firearms because they don't even know that there are any new ones. And you know what else? We need to get more clients."

"More clients? Are you fucking high? We haven't even worked with our current clients; we don't need to bring in more."

Noah understands but still wants to get his hands a bit dirtier. After Raymond passed, he had a change of perspective when it came to the business, and now he's all in.

"Oh, by the way, I'm going to California for a couple of days next week," Noah says. "We're visiting her brother, Adam, and he has a beach house."

"A beach house in California? How the hell did he manage to make that happen after being raised in Philadelphia?"

"He is a director at his advertising agency. One of the best in the business, according to Molly."

"That doesn't add up. All of the thriving ad agencies are in Manhattan." Leo says.

"The original agency is in New York, and I think it's called Doner or something like that. Adam works from the West Coast division. Do you remember that ad for the tootsie pops? With the owl?"

"Of course, everybody does. That was a while back ago, wasn't it?" Leo asks.

"Well, Adam's company did that one."

Leo smiles and asks, "So, this brother-in-law of yours is quite the adman, huh?"

Leo gives Noah a specific look; Noah recognizes it instantly. Through the years, Noah has studied the eyes his brother would give him. The look he's giving Noah in this particular case is his least favorite, and it means that he is plotting something, which is never a good sign.

"You're giving me that look. What the hell are you thinking?"

"Look, Russo Santino hasn't been doing the best lately. Not many people have been going. We need the financial stability to increase, or else our alibi will be invalid. Some advertisement from one of the best admen in the business wouldn't hurt."

A million triggers in Noah's head go off. "No! Fuck no! Fuck you! That's not going to happen!"

Noah has no clue how intense the volume he's speaking at is, but everybody else in the diner does. Mrs. Bambino rushes over and slaps Noah in the back of the head and asks, "What is the matter with you, Noah? This is a family diner. If you'd like to talk like a sailor, do it out at sea. Not in my diner!"

Leo, being the annoying brother he is, says, "That's exactly right. Mrs. Bambino, I couldn't agree more. Noah, what do you have to say to Mrs. Bambino?"

Noah, giving Leo a look that says, 'fuck you, you fucking piece of shit asshole,' sighs and says, "I'm sorry, Mrs. Bambino. It'll never happen again."

Mrs. Bambino smiles and starts rubbing the back of Noah's head that she smacked. "You know I hate coming down on you like that. Carry on."

After she walks away, Noah whispers, "You fucking dickhead. Why the fuck would I let you tie in my brother into the loop of this business? Too risky."

"Too risky? What the fuck are you talking about? Noah, what business do you think we are gonna involve him in? He's advertising a nice steak, not nice narcotics. How is that risky?"

Noah says, "Let's say we get busted."

Leo slaps him right across his face, drawing attention to the table once again. "Don't you dare fucking talk like that again!"

It's not a rule or a requirement, but one of the worst things you can do in the district business around district people is mentioning the idea of getting caught. It makes you not only look weak, but it makes people think that there is something stupid that you're doing, that you know it is stupid, that you know it could lead you into a search warrant. Search warrants aren't terminal for districts because they store everything in a particular place, Alfredo's, but it's unwanted attention from the feds coming their way.

"We aren't getting caught? Do you fucking understand that? We are not getting caught! If you think that we are getting caught, then you shouldn't be in this business. And if you say that in front of somebody other than me, they'll think we're weak. They'll think that we think that we're getting caught, which would make them want to terminate our partnerships."

"Jesus Christ, stop being such a fucking baby. Al Capone got caught."

That actually isn't true, but neither of them paid any attention in history class, so they didn't know any better. Capone was never actually "caught", and he went to jail for tax evasion in 1931.

"It doesn't fucking matter. You don't talk with that mindset."

"Then let me at least finish this hypothetical. We get caught. They look more into it and find out that Russo Santino was just a source of money laundering. They look even more into it and see that Doner advertised for the restaurant, and that looks bad on them, and especially Adam."

"Since when have you given a rat's ass about Adam. Adam this. Adam that. Next thing you know, you're naming your child after the bastard."

Leo sees the angry face on Noah slowly transition into a face reflecting a feeling of sorrow. Noah is usually a sad camper, so a tragic look on his face was never a shock. But, due to the context, Leo knows that something is wrong.

"What's with the look? Did she abort it or something?"

"No, she didn't abort it," Noah lets out with a sigh. "I thought of an official name for my baby, and it's not Adam. But, you're not going to like it."

Leo laughs and says, "Just tell me. It's not like it's my baby; it's yours. C'mon, just tell me."

"It's Raymond. My son's name will be Raymond."

Noah doesn't know what to expect from Leo, and he doesn't know what Leo will pull. But, despite whatever Noah's contemplating, Leo smiles, and it's not an evil smile or a smirk; it's just a smile.

"Noah, I feel so fucking bad for you. For thirty years, you let our father use you like a rag to wipe the dirt off of his shoes. He's a crook, and you can't tell me otherwise. Are you seriously having your son share the name of that man?"

Noah responds, "I've been having fucking nightmares. After I shot that hooker, I saw this weird vision of her dead body in my bathtub. So, I stopped having affairs, and they went away. After you killed him, I've been getting these visions of Raymond floating around in my bathtub. I think if I name my son after him, the visions will go away."

"What the fuck do you think this is? A fucking horror novel? No! It's not. That's not how this shit works. Fuck you and fuck this. If you hate your son that much, then fine! Name him after that piece of shit."

Leo gets up from his chair and takes out his wallet. "Where did that smile go? C'mon Leo, sit down. You're making a scene."

"Oh, I'm making a scene? You're making a big fucking mistake. You have some nerves. My only nephew will be named after the only thing I hate more than the feds." Leo says as he drops some cash on the table.

Leo never storms off without a place to go. After he leaves Bambino's, he goes up to the payphone, and he pushes two quarters in and dials in a number that belongs to Mario's place of business.

An employee picks up and says, "This is Alfredo's."

"Yeah, is Mario there?" Leo asks.

"Yes, he's in his office."

"Tell him I'm coming. My name is Leo." Leo says before he hangs up.

Leo burns rubber and gets to Alfredo's in a flash. When Leo enters, Mario greets him with a hug and a smile. "Leo, how are you doing?"

"Great. Just great. Mind if we have a word in your office? It's about this game of poker of mine."

Mario nods, knowing that it is time for business, and a poker game is never to be ignored. So, he escorts Leo to his office and locks the door. "What's going on, Leo?"

"I need the accounts. The files, or whatever they're called."

"The files for the clients?"

"Yes, bingo. Do you have them? Are you able to whip them up?" Leo asks.

"Yeah, they are in my cabinet. Just give me a second to unlock it." Mario responds. He grabs the key to the cabinet and gets down on his knees, which kills his back.

"Hey, I think I'm ready to go out with that Maria of yours. If that's ok with you, that is."

"Oh, of course. After I get these files, I'll give you her number. She actually just asked me the other day if I had anybody for her. Looks like I have some good news to report."

Mario opens up the cabinet with the key and takes out a rack of files. Each file has the surname of whoever he is keeping the files for at the top. He sorts them alphabetically. He pulls out the one labeled "SANTINO" and hands it to Leo.

"You have a good set of clients. Keep it that way."

"If only it was that easy. I didn't go to business school; I don't really know how sales work."

"It's not about sales; it's about consistency. You check up on them and record. The recording is key, according to your father."

"Recording? Recording what?"

"Gimme that file," Mario says.

Leo hands him the file, and Mario flips it open. He goes to the first page and shows it to Leo. "Look at this. This is how it's done. Do you see this line right here?"

9/16/77 (1 pound) - 11/24/77 (1 pound) - 2/14/78 (½ pound) - 3/10/78 (2 pounds) - 6/10/78 (no sale, ½ left, check back in next month) - 7/30/78 (2 pounds) - 10/22/78 (1 pound) - 12/02/78 (1 pound)

"It shows the date of which his last sale was and exactly how much coke he sold. He records the amount of time it takes for this particular client and builds arithmetic. If it takes two months for these guys to take down one pound, then it would take about half of that time for half of a pound, and it would take double that time to take down double that amount. Do you see where I'm going with this?"

"Yes. But, do you call before you go in?"

"No," Mario answers. "No call. You just show up. These are relatively brief meetings. You show up and ask if they need any more, and if they do, you ask how much and then leave. If they don't, you just leave. Simple as that. But, because this is your first interaction with these people, it will probably be a longer meeting."

Leo takes a closer look at the file and sees that it's for a strip club in New Jersey. "This is in Jersey?"

"If that's what it says, then yeah."

"That's fucking terrific. Now I have to drive Noah over there."

"What's so bad about that?"

"I'm not too happy with him. We got into an intense argument earlier."

"An intense argument? About what?"

"He's naming his son after Raymond," Leo says. "I know that doesn't sound bad, but it is, and don't ask why."

"I won't," Mario says.

Leo shakes his hand and says, "I appreciate you, Mario. I really do. You have been so good to Noah and me for the past week, and I really feel accepted in the group."

"We are thrilled to have you on board. You're going to do great."

Leo and Mario give each other a friendly hug. "Do you mind if I use your phone? I want to tell Noah about the gig."

"In code, I should hope."

"Do you even have to ask?"

"Yeah, go ahead. Just don't make it a long call. The bills are through the roof." Mario requests.

"It'll be brief," Leo says. He goes up to the phone and dials in a number, and he waits and waits for an answer.

On the other side of the call, Molly says, "Molly Santino."

Leo, who is surprised, quickly says, "Hey Molly. It's Leo. How are you doing?"

"Oh, I'm ok. The baby has been kicking like Bruce Lee all day."

"Yeah, Noah told me all about little Raymond."

"Oh, he did? That's nice, and we've actually decided to just call him Ray for short. What do you think of that?"

"I prefer Ray, quite frankly. Is Noah with you?"

"No, I thought the two of you were out at that diner."

"We were, but I left a bit early. I had to go to the restaurant and check some stuff out."

"Oh. He hasn't shown up yet; he probably went to pick up those groceries I requested. Can I help you with anything else?"

"Yeah. Please let him know that tomorrow there is a poker convention in Jersey that we were invited to? Tell him I'll get him at noon."

"Tomorrow? That won't work. We have an appointment with our gynecologist around noon."

"There'll be many more of those. You can just catch him up to speed when he gets back, and I'll even take us all out to a nice steak dinner."

Molly sighs and says, "Leo, no offense, but I think that my husband prioritizes our baby over some poker game."

A devious smile appears on Leo's despicable face. "Oh, absolutely. But, could you just tell him about it for me? I want him to know so that he doesn't feel sad when he finds out I went without him, you know what I mean?"

"I'll definitely let him know. Thanks, Leo."

"Thank you. Also, you never said yes or no to that steak dinner tomorrow night. My treat."

"We'll be there," Molly assures.

Leo knows that he will be driving to New Jersey tomorrow afternoon, and he knows that Noah would be in the passenger seat.

Another rule of the district business is that "poker games" are absolutely mandatory. It doesn't matter if your dad is dead or your wife is giving birth; you must attend every poker game.

Later that night, the two start snuggling on the couch and watch *Cornfields in Texas.* "You know, I've never really liked this show."

"Your dad suggested it." Molly replies.

"My dad had terrible taste. I remember we'd watch the worst shows whenever he'd teach us how to play poker."

"Oh, that reminds me," Molly says as she starts to laugh. "Leo wanted to let you know that there is a huge poker meeting tomorrow afternoon. I told him about the gynecologist, and he insisted I told you anyway."

Noah's eyes pop wide open. "Ah, geez. I'm sorry, Molly. I have to go to this; it's probably with our suppliers."

"What? Are you serious? We have an important appointment with the gynecologist."

"No offense, hon. But, every appointment is important. You can just tell me what the gynecologist says, ok? This is important; I have to make a good impression on these guys."

"Noah, I can't believe we are even having this conversation. Do you know how embarrassing and humiliating it would be for me to be a pregnant woman alone in that waiting room?"

"Honey, this is silly," Noah says. "You are putting your humiliation over the success of my business."

"No, I'm putting our child over the success of your stupid poker game. I thought you'd do the same."

"It's not just a fucking poker game. It's building an impression on these people. Leo and I have to create a persona that is to their liking. This is how we make good relationships. And baby, it's just an appointment, and it's not like you're giving birth. Ok?"

"Oh, fuck you, Noah! Fuck you!"

It's extremely rare for Molly to curse. She grew up in a very polite household; a cuss word is a guaranteed punishment. Molly is the type of gal who will never drink too much and never get into any fights.

"Molly, what has gotten into you?"

"What has gotten into you? You put work before family, and we don't even have a family yet! Get out of my house!"

"Your house? Your house? Are you kidding? If it weren't for me, you'd be a hostess in Philadelphia and would be dating some retired football player who tore his ACL."

"At least he'd show up to the gynecologist appointments."

"Fuck the gynecologist. There will be more appointments, but there won't be more first impressions. This is what I have to do."

"I've done so much during these months," Molly cries. "Besides the pregnancy itself, I've done so much. I've gotten groceries, I've been planning, and you have just sat on your fat ass and just watched me do all of those things. Just get the fuck out!"

"What the hell am I supposed to do? Do you expect me to carry that baby?"

"I expect you to care about me and how I feel. You always ask about the baby. How is the baby doing? How is the baby doing? How is the baby doing? Why not, how am I doing? I'm the mother; I heard that it was a pretty big factor in the process."

Noah says, "You're just fucking hormonal."

The camel's back is now completely broken. Molly's inner strength from these eight months of pregnancy is now unleashed. Instead of spreading out her palm, she curls her fingers up and makes a fist. She swings her arm around and gives Noah's face a nice punch. Blood drips from his nose faster than water drops from clouds.

"You want me out? I'm out!" Noah says.

He picks up the remote and chucks it into the TV, which shatters the glass. As he does that, Molly sees the father of her child, and she isn't happy about the view. Noah grabs his coat and wallet and then he slams the door.

Noah walks down on the sidewalk and tries to get a taxi driver's attention. He is acting like a typical New Yorker with no place to stay and no place to go.

Noah catches a ride and takes it all of the ways over to a random hotel in Westchester. He gets a nice room for a reasonable price and orders a Philly Cheesesteak from the late-night menu. He also gets a chocolate cake.

Noah flips through channels on the hotel TV until he stumbles upon *Magnificent Massacres*. But, it starts making him think of Molly, and he doesn't want to think about her at all.

Now that he's thinking about Molly, he starts thinking about Leo. He thinks about how terrible they left things in the diner, and he also feels like he let his brother down.

Noah grabs the phone on the coffee table next to the bed and dials in Leo's number. He hopes that Leo picks up, and he does.

"Who is this?" Leo barks from the other line.

"It's your brother. Your brother wants to apologize, so please don't hang up."

"Ay, you know what? I'm sorry, too. I lost my temper, you know how I get when it comes to the thought of that prick."

"Yeah, yeah," Noah says, still a bit annoyed.

"Noah, do you know why I hate him? It's because of how he treated you. You deserve better."

"The past is in the past."

"Indeed. Oh, did Molly tell you about the poker game?"

"Yes, and I will be attending. You just have to pick me up at that hotel near Bambino's."

"Why the hell are you at a hotel?" Leo asks.

"Molly is acting crazier than that chick from that Clint Eastwood film." Noah jokes.

"Pregnancy hormones?"

"I don't doubt it," Noah says. "But, saying that to her is a red flag. She'll punch you square in the face."

"She kicked your ass out to the curb, didn't she." Leo laughs.

"No, I left voluntarily. I'm not even telling her when I'm coming back."

"Jesus, I'm sorry," Leo says.

"It's all cool. I ordered a Philly Cheesesteak and some cake, so the night isn't a total bust."

"Philly and cake? My God, I might have to bust a move down to that hotel room and join you."

"Be my guest. I'm in room forty-five."

"No, I think I'll stay put. I have my silk robe on, NBC rolling, blankets tucked in, and whiskey glass filled to the rim… I'm not moving a muscle."

"Well, get me in the morning in my room. I'll order those pancakes that have chocolate chips baked in, the one's mom used to make."

"If they are just half as good as mom's, I'll be there. Does eight in the morning work?"

"Sounds like a plan. Goodnight."

"Goodnight," Leo says as he hangs up the phone.

Leo and Noah never really say that they love each other, and they do, and they both know they do, too.

In the early morning, Leo goes to Noah's hotel room. They order a large order of chocolate chip pancakes and two hot chocolates to go along with it.

As they eat their pancakes, Leo tries to talk as much business as he can. "It's a nightclub. They like to get loose and high, which is where our product comes in. According to the files, they are our most consistent clients, and smaller quantities."

"Did you bring over the files?" Noah asks as he drenches his pancakes with his maple syrup.

"Yes, I actually did," Leo says as he pops open his briefcase. He takes out a yellow file and hands it to Noah. "This is where we are hitting today. And next month, I'd like to go down to our Connecticut clients."

"Which one are they?"

Leo hands Noah a different file. Noah reads it through and asks, "Guns? I thought you said we shouldn't deal with guns right now."

"No, I said we shouldn't try to get Abruzzo into a partnership," Leo says. "Look at the dates that pops wrote on this file; they haven't purchased firearms since February of seventy-eight."

"Ok, but can we focus on this client that we are meeting today?" Noah asks.

"From what I can tell from this file, they are pretty much just as high as a kite all day and all night. It shouldn't take much convincing to restock." Leo explains.

"Can you imagine pops selling drugs to a bunch of high guys?"

"From what Mario disclosed, he was the best fucker in the business. Mario told me that even Antonio said that pops could've probably made more money in a real business position."

"Do you ever think about that? Like, where would we be today if we gave in to our full potential?"

"Making ten thousand dollars a year in a dead-end job. That's where we would be."

Leo and Noah leave the hotel at around noon and start hitting the road to New Jersey.

Noah asks, "Can I ask you something?"

"Yeah, what's going on?"

"How the fuck do I make up for missing the gynecologist meeting?"

"Just go to the next one," Leo says as he laughs at his joke. "I crack myself up."

"That's funny; you don't make anybody else laugh. I'm fucking serious, and she's really pissed at me."

"She married you; what does she expect? Calm down. It's not the end of the world. We'll go to a nice steak dinner and make everything better."

"She's not the type to be appeased by medium-rare steak

"Well, that's ok. She can get a salad." Leo laughs again, but Noah remains unhappy.

"There's a time for fucking around, but that time isn't now. I want to make things right. We don't fight often; I don't know what to do."

"I'm serious. We'll take her to a nice dinner. Would it make you feel better if we pull over and give her a call from a payphone?"

"It would make me feel better if I could tell her about what I do for a living."

"Well, I'm not the one who told you to marry the first chick who puts out. Pops gave you a warning before you proposed."

"I get it; it's my own fault," Noah sighs. "This is going to sound absolutely terrible, but I've thought about getting myself a girlfriend."

"A girlfriend? My God, you have a kid on the way. I'm sorry, I can condone affairs to an extent, but a significant other?"

Noah knows it's terrible and downright disgusting. But, he is desperate and willing to do what he must to obtain a sense of happiness. Ever since the pregnancy, Molly hasn't been the most passionate partner. Noah wants to have a girlfriend to be the aspect that is absent from his marriage.

"I know, I know. But, give me a break. It's hard to love a girl who won't show you love and who won't emotionally be with you at night."

"I'm going to stop you right there before you continue talking like a chick."

"Fuck this. Wake me up when we arrive at the joint. I'm getting some shut-eye."

"Fine by me." Leo insists.

Leo pulls up to the nightclub at around 12:04PM. He wakes up Noah and says, "Get your shit together. Your eyes are all baggy."

"These are fucking drug addicts. I really doubt that they will care whether or not we have baggy eyes."

"Well, I don't give a fuck about what they do or don't care about. I care about it! This isn't a game of wealth; it's a game of legacy, and wealth just comes along with it. Don't you ever forget that."

To Leo, it's about the legacy, not the money. To Noah, it's about the money, not the legacy. Leo is in it to win it; Noah is in it to cash out.

The nightclub, called Brass Base, is one of the most popular ones in Jersey. The owners, Michael and Steven, have run the place since 1976 and have raked in lots and lots of money. They have no clue what the hell a district is; they just know that they get drugs, and that's all they care about.

Leo and Noah enter the club, which is entirely empty. There are a few custodians that are prepping for the night. Leo walks up to one and asks, "Are Michael and Steven here?"

The Hispanic custodian replies, "Lo siento, no hablo inglés."

Leo asks Noah, "Do you have any clue to what the hell he just said."

"He doesn't speak English," Noah says. "Let's just keep walking around."

The custodian goes back to sweeping up the floor as the boys continue to scavenger across the club, searching for an office of any sort. "Should we holler their names and see if we get a response?" Noah asks.

"No, this isn't like a horror movie. They'll be here; there's no way in hell they'd just leave these custodians with the keys."

Leo spots a door that says 'EMPLOYEES ONLY' and hears loud rock music playing from the room's interior. "Bingo!"

"Ok, so should we just knock on the door?"

"Knock on the door? They are cranking music to such an intense volume that we could have an atomic war in this club, and they wouldn't hear. They wouldn't hear a knock; let's just go in."

"No, it says that it's for employees only."

"Noah, get your head in the game. We sell cocaine to these guys; I'm pretty fucking sure that we are considered employees." Leo says.

Without approval or further discussion, Leo barges into the room and catches the two owners puffing on two blunts. Leo catches Michael off guard. "Holy shit! It's a cop!"

"Relax, I'm not a cop," Leo says. "Neither is my associate. My name is Leonardo Santino."

"Santino? Where have I heard that name before?" Steven asks.

"My father, Raymond Santino, used to be your supplier."

"Oh shit, Raymond! Is he here? He came just in time, too. We are just a week away from being bone dry."

"Actually, Raymond passed not too long ago. My brother, Noah, and I will be taking care of you guys from now on."

"Oh, please sit down. Michael, go get these two beers." Steven orders.

"Oh, I'll pass. I'm driving back, so I'll stay sober. So will my brother."

"Can't we get you guys something else?" Michael asks.

"If you guys have Sprite, that would be perfect. No problem if you don't." Leo says.

"And for you, Noah?" Michael asks.

"If he's getting Sprite, I'll take Coke," Noah says.

"Wow, you're quite the tiger, aren't you? Coming right up." Steven says as he walks to the back of the room.

"So, you're running low on the white stuff, huh?" Leo asks.

"Look, I don't know how you plan on running things, but this is how this shit goes," Michael says as he takes a massive wad of cash from his pocket. "You're going to put us down for two pounds, take this cash, and never show up unannounced like that again."

"I thought that my old man did the same thing?"

"No, he would knock on the door. He would always knock. Never just barge in here, or I might pull out a gun as a reflex because I take you as a fed. Do you see where I'm getting with this?"

"I'm sorry, I just figured that as your suppliers, we are employees also. But, message received."

"Good."

Steven returns to the couch with a glass bottle of Sprite and a black tray with two lines of cocaine and a white straw next to them. "Here is your Sprite," Steven says as he hands it to Leo. Steven puts the black tray in front of Noah and says, "And your coke."

"Woah, Woah, Woah. You must've misinterpreted. I wanted Coca-Cola. Not cocaine."

"Well, fuck that. You expect us to let those lines go to waste?"

"I'd feel terrible snorting what I'm selling. You're offering what we are here to supply."

"Oh, that's what is holding you back? C'mon, we're happy to spare two lines."

"Ok, truth be told: it's just not my lifestyle."

"Lifestyle? Are you saying we are scum? That this lifestyle we are living is so terrible?" Steven barks.

"No, no, no. You have it all wrong. It's not a bad lifestyle; it's just not mine."

"He thinks that he's superior to us just because he's clean," Steven says to Michael.

Noah, wanting to make this sale so desperately, grabs the straw and puts one of the ends up his nose. He puts the bottom of the straw at the start of the line of cocaine, and then he takes a deep breath as he thinks to himself, *two lines won't kill you*, Noah. He snorts the whole line of cocaine up his left nostril and then, as fast as he can, moves to the other line and sniffs that one up, too.

Two seconds later, Noah's brain feels a sensation that it has never felt before. Noah has been the assistant for thirty years, but now he feels like he's the top dog. Noah now feels superior to Leo, which is unheard of from him. It takes about ten seconds for him to finally spit out, "See. No disrespect."

Noah starts rubbing his nose and sweating intensely. "Well, everything is settled then, and you should be receiving your package by Wednesday."

After they get into New York, the boys pull over at a gas station to give Molly a ring. As Noah dials in the number, Leo asks, "What was it like?"

Noah finishes dialing Molly's home number and asks, "What are you talking about?"

"The cocaine. What was it like?"

Noah smiles and says, "It's a feeling unlike any other. Hold on, the phone is ringing.

Molly picks up and asks, "Hello?"

"Hey honey, please don't hang up."

"Oh, Noah, I was so worried about you. About last night, I'm so sorry. Can we move past it?"

"Absolutely. I'm sorry, too, and let's just act like it never happened. How was the appointment?"

"Standard." Molly answers.

"Well, Leo offered to take us both out for a steak dinner. Are you in?"

"Sure, let me slip something nice on."

"Ok, we'll be there in a little bit," Noah says, and then he hangs up.

At dinner, Noah kisses Molly's ass like never before; he knows that she's still bitter about him skipping the appointment for a poker game. Molly isn't making a big fuss about it because her gynecologist told her that it's essential to keep a calm and relaxing mindset.

Noah browses through the menu and then says, "The lobster sounds phenomenal. I haven't had lobster in ages."

"Well, order whatever you want. Whether it's a lobster or a steak, it's my treat." Leo insists.

"Leo, you are so kind. What's the occasion?" Molly asks.

"I'd just like to celebrate your baby. In fact, let me propose a toast." Leo says as he raises his glass. "To Ray Santino."

Noah smiles and says, "Leo, I'm not going to lie to you. You saying that means the world to me. To us."

Leo smiles at his brother, letting him know that he's supportive of him naming his son after the father they both despise. They all set their drinks down.

Leo takes out his box of Old Port cigars and whips one out, and places it in his mouth. He asks Noah, "Do you want one?"

Noah sighs and says, "No thanks. You see, the smell of cigar smoke makes Molly feel nauseous."

Leo takes out his lighter, but before he lights, Noah gives him an obviously loud cough saying, take a hint. Leo, not understanding, proceeds to light his cigar. Noah says, "Uh, Leo. Cigar smoke from my mouth smells no different than cigar smoke from yours."

Leo, after a lot of blatant hints, finally understands. He puts his cigar away and says, "This is nice. I treat you to a nice steak dinner, and you treat me to the dissatisfaction of not puffing on my cigar."

"Leo, I'm sorry. Ever since Molly got pregnant, I've had to do certain things that I used to do around her, outside."

"I'm just giving you a hard time. Speaking of hard times, we have to do something about Russo Santino."

Molly asks, "What's wrong with the restaurant?"

Noah steps in and says, "Well, don't freak out...but Russo Santino hasn't been doing the best lately."

"We need to step up our game. Marco and I want to get an advertising agency to do something for us, but it's so expensive. My God."

"Did Noah not tell you about my brother?"

Leo smiles, and Noah sees where he's going with his spiel. Leo, knowing the answer, asks, "What about your brother?"

"Well, he works for one of the biggest ad agencies in the world; it's called Doner. He'd be happy to do an ad for you guys."

"Molly, that's so nice. Thank you so much." Leo says as he leans over to give Molly a kiss on the cheek.

"No. Molly, we wouldn't want to mix family with business, would we?" Noah points out.

"Noah, my brother would do this for us. It's no problem." Molly assures.

The waiter comes by and asks, "Can I get you guys any drinks?"

Molly goes first and says, "Just water, please."

Noah says, "I'll take a scotch on the rocks."

Leo says, "I'll take an absolut martini. Wait, scratch that. I'd feel bad drinking alcohol in front of you while you're pregnant, Molly. I'll just have water, please."

Molly smiles and says, "That's so sweet."

Feeling manipulated by his manipulative brother, Noah tells the waiter, "You know what, scratch the scotch."

Later that night, Leo goes to Jimmy Jr. Colombo's nightclub to have a couple of drinks. Colombo's lounge isn't exactly his; it is his and his brother's. His brother isn't in the district business; he's in the club business. However, he is well aware of what goes on.

Leo starts eating the wings that he ordered from the midnight menu. Leo starts feeling like complete crap only ten minutes after eating the wings, so he goes to the bathroom.

When he comes out, he spots Noah from the other side of the club, shaking Colombo's hand. Before he can spot Leo, he exits the club.

Leo goes up to Colombo and asks, "What was Noah doing here?"

Colombo says, "He wanted to thank me for being a part of this deal you guys just made."

Leo buys it, not knowing that Noah walks out of that club with two small baggies of the white stuff.

He looks over to Colombo and sees that his nose is bleeding. "Jimmy, your nose is bleeding."

"Ah shit, thanks for telling me," Colombo says as he grabs a rag to wipe the blood off of his nose. "Some people don't even mention it to me."

"Does it happen often?" Leo asks.

"Every now and then. It's what happens when you snort coke as much as I do."

"Noah snorted two lines today at the business meeting."

"No kidding."

"Can I ask you something? It might be personal, so you don't have to answer the question. How do you know when you're addicted to coke?"

"To tell you the truth, it's quite evident. You're addicted when you flip your wires."

CHAPTER 7:

LET'S SETTLE THIS

Noah has risen.

Molly is due in two weeks, and she is thinking of ways to prepare herself and Noah for the delivery mentally. They know what to do with their baby; they just don't know what to teach him.

Molly is Jewish, Noah is Catholic. Molly's parents have been getting on Noah's tail about the baby's religion ever since he was conceived. Noah, wanting to represent his father as much as possible, insists on Ray getting baptized.

Noah made a compromise after that fight, which would lead to Adam being the godfather of their baby. He was not aware that Judaism doesn't have godfathers, so that idea was quickly resolved.

Noah wants Molly to convert to Catholicism, but she refuses. She is invested in her religion, and she says that if Noah claims that it's no big deal to alter beliefs, he should convert for her.

Noah and Molly go into the baby's room with two buckets of paint: light yellow and dark orange.

Noah wants it to be orange so that the baby will learn to love the color. It was also Raymond's favorite, but Molly doesn't know that.

Like a typical mother, Molly thinks that the walls should be comfortable for the baby's eyes and that orange is too dominant of a color.

"I've never met anybody with an orange room. That's such a terrible color for a room. You don't notice light yellow, and it's soothing to the naked eye; orange is so noticeable."

"Of course, it's noticeable; it's painted all over the walls. If you want people not to notice the color of your walls, then invite Stevie Wonder over for dinner. For crying out loud, it's just a color." Noah says.

"When you walk into a room that is shaded with light blue, you don't think about it. You're not thinking about the color of the wall. With the color orange, you are thinking, why is this room orange?"

Noah smiles and kisses Molly on the cheek and says, "I guess you're right."

She smiles and kisses him back, saying, "I always am."

Noah lets it slide, using all of his power not to give her a rude response, which is what he loves to do for kicks.

Noah wakes up to the sound of his wife on the phone with her father, who he can't stand.

Nathan Hoffman, Molly's father, is a man made out of respect and pride. He served in the Second World War, and now he waves the American flag up in the air every day. He is currently a cop in Philly.

When Nathan first met Noah, which was near their senior year in high school, he was impressed. Not because of Noah himself, it was because of Raymond's success.

Noah never necessarily had a problem with Nathan. But, when it came time for Noah to propose, he asked Nathan for his blessing, and Nathan immediately declined and said, "If you'd like to marry my daughter, you'll have to go through with it without my blessing."

Noah asked why that was, and he answered, saying, "My daughter has worked hard for everything she has. You didn't buy your house; your father did. You don't have money coming in, your father does, and some of it goes to you."

This was before Noah and Leo were acting managers of Russo Santino, back when Raymond was trying to figure out whether or not they were ready, but we all know that it wasn't the restaurant Raymond was worried about at the time.

At Noah and Molly's wedding, Nathan wasn't very blissful. He walked her down the aisle because his wife, Maya, made him.

Ever since the two have always called each other out whenever an opportunity approached. So suffice to say, Noah and Nathan have bad blood.

Nathan asks, "So, how are you feeling? Any pain? Is it hurting?"

"I wouldn't say I'm in pain; I'm just in a constant state of being uncomfortable. I don't like how I look in all of my maternity clothes."

Noah gives his input, "Honey, you look beautiful in everything you wear. I'm serious."

Nathan hears Noah's voice from the other line. Nathan laughs and says, "Molly, is that Noah I hear?"

"Yes, I think we woke him up," Molly says. "Would you like to say hi to him?"

Noah freaks and nonverbally tells her not to hand him the phone. But it's too late. Nathan smiles from his living room and says, "Nothing would delight me more; put him on."

She smiles and hands Noah the phone, which makes him very unhappy. Noah sighs and says, "Hey, Nathan. How are things in Philly?"

"Better than how things are in New York. Why don't you move that little steakhouse of yours to Philadelphia?"

"I'd rather live in New York and wake up in the morning without having to shovel snow," Noah says to spite Nathan, who is having the time of his life on the other end of the call.

Nathan knows that Noah is trying to be an ass, so he says, "Molly filled me in on the whole gynecologist fiasco. I find it interesting that you put poker over your baby."

"Nathan, I know that you live off of naval benefits and don't know how business works, so let me tell you that these poker meets are important for morale," Noah says.

"I may not be in business, but I know that family always comes first. I'm a cop; it seems like you forget that sometimes. I put my family before work because work isn't everlasting. Don't you agree?"

"You see, my philosophy differs slightly. Family is before business, but this wasn't a situation where I had to put family first, and it was just a gynecologist meeting. No harm, no foul."

"Maybe you ought to read one of those parenting books."

"I already have. You can ask your daughter for clarification. And while you're at it, why don't you have a great rest of your day, Nathan."

"I prefer Mr. Hoffman."

"That's great. I prefer Nathan." Noah says as he aggressively hangs up the phone.

"One of these days, I wish the two of you could just get along. I don't want Ray's father and grandfather to hate each other."

"I'm sorry, Molly. I truly am. I don't want to hate him either; he just makes it so fucking easy. He's insulting me. He doesn't think I'm fit to be your child's father or even your husband. He acts like he is the king of the hill, but the only thing that he is the king of is shoveling snow."

Noah, furious, storms out of the bedroom and into his bathroom. He locks the door, so Molly can't enter to comfort him. Noah turns on the faucet, and bathwater starts pouring out.

He goes to the cupboard above the sink and opens it up. Inside, a small brown cigar box of Glens stands. He takes the cigar box and opens it up. Noah quit smoking cigars a week ago, so why does he still have a cigar box? It's where he stores his cocaine. One might think that it's absurd to keep illicit recreational drugs in a blatant cigar box with no lock. However, Noah knows that Molly won't even go near the box because of how disgusted she is by the smell. It's like hiding gold from Superman using a box made out of Kryptonite.

Noah removes the small baggie of cocaine out of the box and takes the twist tie off. He dumps a small amount onto the counter and uses his razor blade to cut the cocaine into two lines.

Noah reaches back into the cigar box and takes out his straw. He slides it a bit up his right nostril and places the straw at the end of the line. Noah closes his eyes and scrunches his face; he wants it, but he's nervous.

He does the first line but then stops before the second. *I'm crazy*, Noah says to himself. He puts the straw back down on the counter and looks back into the mirror. He doesn't see himself in the reflection, but Raymond.

"Did you think you could do it? You're a coward. You always have been, and you always will be." Raymond taunts.

"I have a kid on the way, and I'd like to be a good father. Maybe you can take some notes."

"Noah, stop; you're hurting my feelings," Raymond says sarcastically. "Although, I do appreciate you naming your son after me. But, I'm not even close to forgiving you."

"I'm not looking for your forgiveness; I just want you to stop bugging me. You're ruining my life, and you're not even in it."

Noah is going crazy. He's talking to his reflection and sees it as Raymond. Noah knows that he's crazy and that Raymond is just a figment of his hallucinations, but he still feels obligated to respond to his deceased father.

"You better be looking for forgiveness. You watched your brother kill me. You had a gun pointed right at his skull but didn't pull? Why is that? I'll tell you why; it's because you're a fucking coward. It's the same reason why you didn't snort those lines." Raymond says.

Noah screams, "Fuck you!" He grabs his straw and puts it up to his right nostril, and snorts the line of cocaine in a matter of seconds. After he does, he drops the straw, raises his head from the counter, and looks into the mirror. He looks at Raymond, who is smiling. Noah swings back his arm and smashes his fist into the mirror.

The pieces of shattered glass fall off the mirror and onto the counter. Noah looks at his cut and bloody hand, and he screams. "Son of a bitch!"

Noah starts to cry. Molly screams from the bedroom, "What is going on?"

Noah knows that she'll use the key to get into the bathroom if she doesn't respond. He grabs the baggie of cocaine and ties it back up with the twisty. He shoves the baggie into his cigar box and puts it back into the cupboard, doing all of this with his left hand.

To himself, "Fuck, fuck, fuck, fuck, fuck!" Noah nearly cries in pain but keeps it together. His high isn't kicking in yet, which he is desperately desiring right now.

He runs across the master bathroom and opens up the door with his left hand. Molly barges in with dear concern. "What happened? Who are you talking to?"

She notices the bloody hand and automatically goes into nurse mode, even though she only has hostess work experience. "What did you do? Come over to the sink. I think we still have some in the cupboard."

They move over to the sink. She grabs Noah by his right wrist and presses it onto the counter, putting his bloody hand over the sink.

"Still have what in the cupboard?"

"The rubbing alcohol," Molly says as she takes out the small bottle. She unscrews the top and says, "You are going to feel a slight sting."

"How slight of a sting?" Noah asks.

Too late! Molly pours the rubbing alcohol all over Noah's cuts. The excruciating pain takes over his body immediately, and it leads to him screaming in pain. He shouts, "Ok! Ok! That's enough! That's enough! Stop pouring! That's enough!"

Noah tries to move his hand, but Molly has it completely pinned to the counter. Noah feels the pain spreading throughout his body, and then he feels it slowly fade. His cocaine high is kicking in. He starts to think, *why am I taking this shit?* Noah, without thinking thoroughly, uses the back part of his hand to smack the side of his wife's face.

"What the hell is the matter with you?" Molly asks.

"When I say that's enough, it means that's enough," Noah shouts, no longer feeling any pain in his right hand. "I'm getting out of here."

Noah gets out of the bathroom and into his bedroom, leaving Molly in the bathroom in awe. Noah browses through his closet in search of his dark green buttoned shirt. Noah hollers to Molly, "Ay, where is that green shirt that I like so much?"

She doesn't respond. For the first time in their marriage, Molly feels like she made the wrong choice at the altar. Molly looks at Noah and sees an entirely different person. She isn't looking at Noah; she's looking at Raymond.

Noah finds his green shirt on the floor of his closet and shouts, "I'm out to the hospital. I shouldn't be gone for a long time."

Noah starts to exit the room and sees his wife cowardly crouched in the corner of the bathroom. "I'll call you after I'm out, ok?"

"You hit me, Noah. You slapped me right across my face." Molly cries with tears rushing.

"Hey, I begged you to stop, and I couldn't have begged any harder. Now you know for next time, ok?"

"I don't even know who you are," Molly says, trying to keep herself together. Usually, she would be cursing right now. But, she's in too much shock to even contemplate a proper reaction. "What has gotten into you?

What is making him act so bizarre? Why isn't he the good guy that he is? What is changing his ways? What has gotten into him? The answer…cocaine.

Meanwhile, at Russo Santino, it's a decent crowd for the afternoon. Out of the hundred tables, about a fourth are taken. Marco sits in his office, which is a private room that rich people reserve for special occasions. It's also where the heads gather to play cards, puff cigars and enjoy life. It's mainly used for meetings between Henry and Raymond, but now it's for Marco and the brothers.

Marco enjoys running the restaurant, and he spends most of his time there, and Marco conducts his district business there. Like right now, he is looking at a sheet of paper with columns and rows.

He looks at another slip of paper that says:

Brass Base Nightclub. 1200 Princeton Ave, Jersey City, NJ 551. Two pounds.
Supplier is Colombo.
BY WEDNESDAY!!

Marco copies the notes down into his columned paper, along with many other addresses and orders. Another box has Pete Abruzzo as the supplier, and Marco thinks to himself, *man, oh man, I wish we had him in the group.*

After Marco writes it down, he hears a scream of a young kid from the main dining area. *What the hell was that,* Marco asks himself.

Five minutes earlier, in the restaurant's main dining area, a waiter, Bryan, is taking a party of 5's order: a grandmother, a grandfather, a father, a mother, and a kid.

An old lady says, "Oh, and for me, I'll have a decaf coffee."

"Alright, it's all coming right up," Bryan says as he jots the order down.

He walks away from the table and spots the busboy, Eric, wiping down a table just used by customers who just left. Bryan approaches and asks, "Do you have a second?"

"Yeah, what do you need?" Eric asks.

"Can you whip up four coffees for table twenty-one? One is decaf; the others are just regular. Can you do that for me?"

"Yeah, no problem. When you say that one is decaf, is that excluding the four coffees or including?"

"Including, I would do it myself, but the bartenders are out, and I need to whip up an absolut martini."

"Don't worry about it. I'll get right on it." Eric says.

"Thank you very much," Bryan says as he goes behind the bar to make the martini.

Eric finishes cleaning the table and puts the rag back in his pocket. After he finishes up, he heads into the kitchen to make the four coffees.

Eric grabs a circular tray and places it next to the regular coffee pot. He reaches under the counter, grabs four mugs by the handles, and puts them around the tray. He holds the regular coffee pot and pours it into three cups, about four-fifths full. He sets it down and then picks up the decaf pot, and he pours it into the empty mug and then sets it back down.

He grabs the end of the tray and puts his hand underneath the tray. He takes it off the counter, let's go with his left hand, holds it from the bottom center with his right palm, and raises it to his ear level. He carefully exits the kitchen and heads back out into the main dining area.

Eric is the best busboy at Russo Santino. He is just entering his first summer after high school graduation; he's a straight-A student. His parents don't have the money for his dream school, Columbia. So, he is working his ass off to make enough money to attend.

When he gets close to the table, he starts to lower the tray so that it's at a place where his right arm can reach the mugs. But that doesn't do much when you trip on your untied shoelaces.

Eric trips and lets the tray of mugs filled with burning hot liquid drop on the table. All of the coffee goes on the young kid's stomach. He screams and cries in agonizing pain. Eric panics and says, "Oh my God! Oh my God! I'm so sorry! It was an accident!"

The father shouts, "No shit, it was an accident! That doesn't matter!"

The mother asks her grandma, "Mom, you're the nurse. What do we do?"

The grandma quickly answers, "The most important thing to do right now is removing the affected clothing. Unbutton his shirt."

The mother starts to unbutton her son's shirt quickly. "Mommy, it burns! It hurts so much!"

"I know, Honey. I know. It's going to be ok, and we're going to get you to the hospital. Stay strong for mommy."

Marco rushes over to the table to see the mother removing the shirt from the child's body. "What happened over here?"

The father yells, "You're brilliant busboy dropped a whole tray of coffee onto my son's shirt!"

"Jesus, I'm so sorry; I'll call an ambulance," Marco says. "Eric, follow me."

Eric follows Marco, who is running to the hostess table. The hostess is reviewing the sheets for the reservations for that night, and it's filled. The Doner ad is reeling in customers to the restaurant.

Marco says to the hostess, "Henrietta, call an ambulance. This kid is severely burned from hot coffee. After you call the ambulance, give Leo and Noah a ring."

"Right away, sir." Henrietta says as she dials in 9-11.

Eric says to Marco, "My God, I'm so sorry. Mr. Russo, you have to know it was an accident, and I tripped on my shoelace."

"Are you telling me that you served a tray of drinks, nevertheless hot ones, with untied shoes? I would've never expected this from you. You're our best guy."

"I know, I know, and I can't begin to tell you how stupid I feel. First thing tomorrow, I'm buying unlaced shoes. This will never happen again."

"Eric, I pity you. You're a good kid with a bad life. But, you're fired, and it's as simple as that."

"This is my first mistake. Name another mistake I've made." Eric points out.

"I don't have to name another mistake when this current mistake is going to cost us big time. Forget about the bad publicity; think about all of the lawsuits, and they might not even accept a settlement."

"Mr. Russo, you have my word. I will never do anything like this again. I promise."

"You're right. You won't. It's because you're not going to work here anymore."

"I need this job."

"I need you to leave. You're a good kid, but you're fired, and that's business."

Leo is in his bed and eating two pieces of toast slathered with butter as he watches the morning news. He still has a headache from drinking so much the previous night at a concert.

His phone rings; Henrietta is calling from the restaurant. Leo grabs his phone and answers, "It's Leonardo."

"Hey, it's Henrietta."

"Who the hell is Henrietta?" Leo asks.

"The hostess at your restaurant. I've been here for like two months. Don't you remember?"

"I do now. What's going on?" Leo asks.

"There's an emergency, and Eric spilled coffee on a kid, and now he's getting rushed to the hospital in an ambulance."

"That can't be right. Eric is too smart. It must've been that Anthony kid who threw up on the head chef."

"No, it was Eric. He's fired."

"Jesus Christ, Eric actually did it. How badly is he burned?" Leo asks.

"I'm not sure, but I know that it's pretty bad. I mean, he's a kid that just had coffee dumped on him."

"Is Marco down there?"

"He's the one who told me to call." Henrietta answers.

"Alright, I'm on my way. Tell Marco that I'll be there soon. Do you want me to call Noah?"

"No, just get down here."

Molly is crying on the phone with Adam, "He hit me. He didn't even say sorry."

"What did he say?" Adam asks as he sips his pineapple juice by his pool.

"I don't remember. He reiterated that it was my fault because I didn't stop when he told me to. And then he said something like, "now you know for next time.""

"My Lord, I'm so sorry. Noah is a fucking asshole, and I shouldn't have done that ad for him."

"No, he's not an asshole. He was just in pain. He was caught up in the moment, and he wasn't thinking straight."

"Even when a man isn't thinking straight, he has no right to resort to physical acts of violence. I'm going to fly down there and beat the shit out of him. Don't defend him, and he doesn't deserve your defense."

"Adam, promise me that you won't tell dad. Promise me." Molly begs as she wipes the tears off of her eyes with a tissue.

"Molly, would you please let me? If we tell dad, he'll teach Noah a lesson that he will never forget."

"The answer is no. Promise me that you won't tell him. Promise me!" Molly cries.

Adam sighs and says, "Fine, this will just stay between us. But Molly, you have to do something about this. When he comes crawling back, don't let him go without a fight. This is unacceptable. Why did he even punch the mirror in the first place?"

Henrietta calls the home phone from the restaurant. "Hold on, I have another call," Molly says as she answers the other call. "Hello?"

"Is this Noah Santino's home?" Henrietta asks.

"Yes, I'm his wife, Molly. What can I do for you?" Molly asks as she sniffs.

"Is everything ok, ma'am?"

"Oh, everything is fine. I'm sorry, who is this?"

"This is Henrietta; I'm the hostess at Russo Santino. Is Noah around?"

"No, I'm sorry. He's in the hospital. Can I take a message?" Molly asks.

"Why is he in the hospital?" Henrietta asks.

"He cut his hand. I'm sorry, I have my brother on the other line. Is there a message I can leave for him?"

"Do you know when he'll return?"

"No, I don't. Can I take a message or not?" Molly asks impatiently.

"Well, if he returns, then just tell him that we have an emergency down at the restaurant."

"What's going on?" Molly asks.

"A kid got burned with coffee." Henrietta answers.

Leo gets down to the restaurant ten minutes after the phone call. He slips into his best gray suit.

He gets into the restaurant and goes up to the hostess stand. He asks Henrietta, "What's the status?"

"They left for the hospital. They said that they will give us a call when his burn is diagnosed or some shit like that."

"Is my brother on the way?" Leo asks.

"No, his wife said he's in the hospital."

"The hospital? What the fuck is he in the hospital for?"

"Cut his hand. Probably is getting stitches."

"Jesus Christ. Where is Marco?" Leo asks as he takes out a cigar and a match.

"In the private room. He's waiting for you." Henrietta answers.

Leo swipes the end of the match on the table and gives the match a flare. He lights his cigar as he walks to the private room, and he opens it up and sees Marco biting his fingernails anxiously.

Leo asks, "What exactly happened?"

"That spaz didn't tie his fucking shoelaces. How do you carry four mugs of piping hot coffee with untied shoelaces?"

"Is the problem that the coffee is too hot? Like over the normal temperature?" Leo asks.

"No, I checked. It's the same temperature as always."

"Eric couldn't have picked a worse time to do this. This has to happen just when we get back on the map. Just when the advertising pays off. Just when things got good. My God, how the fuck are we going to recover after this? Can't you see the headlines?"

"I see them all. We are so fucked. Just think about the lawsuits."

"Are we going to offer a settlement?" Leo asks.

"Of course, we are going to offer a settlement. We don't want this story to get out to the press; we'll be finished."

"Then why are you so freaked out? We'll offer them the settlement, and nobody else will ever know."

"You didn't see how pissed off the father was. I mean, sure, I'd be pissed off. But I saw it in his eyes. He's going to want to take us down, and it'll have to be a hefty settlement, disregarding the medical bills."

"What degree is the burn?"

"I don't fucking know."

"Well, it might be first degree. That's not so bad, is it?"

"Why does that matter? Any degree is bad publicity."

"So, what do we do while we wait? Should we start making up the settlement?"

"We're not starting the settlement until our lawyer is down here and we get word on the burn severity."

The group partnership shares a lawyer: Ian Kyles, and he mainly works for the restaurant.

"When is Ian getting down here?" Leo asks.

Marco sighs and says, "Any minute. Where's your brother? Is he on the way?"

"No, he's in the hospital. The jackass cut his hand somehow, and now he might need stitches."

"How did he cut his hand?"

"I don't know, Henrietta didn't say. Are we going to visit the kid in the hospital?"

"I think we should. Should we wait for Noah to get back?"

"Who knows how long he could be gone," Leo points out. "I say we act fast. As soon as they give us the status, we are writing a settlement and going down to the hospital."

"Don't you think that it shows a lack of sympathy if we show up to the hospital with a settlement just a couple of hours after the incident?"

"Don't you think we should get this taken care of before any word gets out?"

"We'll see what Ian thinks. Is it even legal to make a settlement that requires the other party not to discuss this with anyone?"

"It should be. One thing is for sure; this is going to dent our financial situation severely. It's going to be around a two-month recession, and that means that we have to take it easy on the money for a while."

Noah exits the hospital at around 2:30 PM with a dozen stitches. He knows that he has to make things right with Molly, even though he doesn't feel obligated to apologize.

Before he tries to catch a cab, he spots a small floral shop. He remembers how Molly told him that daisies are the only flowers she loves the smell of so much.

Noah goes into the floral shop and is automatically disgusted by the overbearing smell of flowers. A lady at the front says, "Welcome to the shop. Can I help you?"

"Yeah, I just need a dozen daisies," Noah says as he takes out his wallet. "Can you fetch some for me?"

The lady picks up a dozen from a basket she has under her desk. "I have one right here. Somebody ordered them and then canceled."

"How much will that cost?" Noah asks.

"Three-fifty. What's the occasion?"

"I pissed off my wife. The flowers are going to appease her, I hope."

"If you want my opinion, flowers are weak. If you want to show them that you are sorry, you should go big."

"Like what?"

The lady smiles and says, "Jewelry."

"Jewelry? That junk is expensive. They don't even look that nice. Waste of money in my eyes."

"Your eyes aren't her eyes. Flowers are easy; you don't have to do much. Jewelry shows you put thought into it."

"I don't think that inanimate objects result in love from my wife, and I think flowers will do," Noah says as he hands her the five-dollar bill.

The lady hands Noah his dollar and fifty cents back. "I couldn't see myself staying mad at my significant other if they blinded my eyes with fancy jewelry."

Noah is now intrigued. He knows now that flowers won't make up for him slapping her in the face. He knows that he has to go big or else she won't let him go home.

"Do you know any jewelry joints around here?" Noah asks.

"There's a nice one down the block, but it's a bit pricey."

"Eh, I can afford it," Noah says, not knowing that a substantial settlement is being conducted at his restaurant.

Molly is laying down on her back on the couch. She knows that a big fight is coming her way, and she knows that she's eventually going to crack and forgive him. Noah has some kind of power over her. But what she can't figure out is why he's suddenly changing? *Why is he acting so cruel?*

She hears the front door unlock and quickly sits back up. Noah enters and immediately tries to apologize. "I'm sorry, Molly. I'm so sorry. It was in the heat of the moment."

Molly recites what her big brother told her, "Even in the heat of the moment, no man should hit his significant other."

"C'mon, hear me out. I cut my hand pretty fucking badly, and I had to get a dozen stitches, a dozen. And you didn't listen to me in the first place."

"So you're putting this all on me?"

"I'm not putting anything on you. But, I get easily frustrated when you disobey me."

"You are not someone that I have to obey or disobey. You are my husband, and you should be the one man that I'm never afraid of."

"Honey, you don't know what you're talking about right now. You're not afraid of me; you're mad at me."

"If I'm not afraid of you, then why am I backing up while you are approaching me? That's not just something I often do, and I'm afraid you might hit me again."

"It felt like you were killing me. It's kind of hard to reason when all you can feel is tremendous pain. You should know that I never would do anything to hurt you intentionally."

"Sure you would. Remember the gynecologist meeting?"

"How could I forget when that's all you talk about all of the time? Why are we still on this?"

"You knew that it hurt me, and you still went to the poker meet. And then all you did was say sorry, and for some reason, I forgave you automatically." Molly says.

"I never said that I was sorry. I never apologized."

"Yes, you did. You called me from the payphone."

"I said that I was sorry that I hurt you, but I never said that I was sorry for what I did. I had no regrets when I made that phone call, and I have no regrets now."

"What are you saying?"

"Let me make this crystal clear to you; I don't regret missing the gynecologist. If I could go back in time, I wouldn't change a thing about that decision. If I could go back in time, I would change a lot about this morning. But that poker meeting was important, and I did what I had to do."

Molly wants to cry, but she doesn't want him to see. She is doing everything she can to bottle up her emotions.

"I remember on Christmas Eve, your mother and I were decorating the tree while you guys smoked on the balcony. She told me that Raymond missed her delivery to attend a meeting. After she told me that, I felt so glad to have a loving husband who would never prioritize anything over me or our family. But now, I don't see that husband, and I see Raymond. To tell you the truth, I'm scared that you'd miss the birth of our baby over a poker meeting."

"Now that's just nonsense."

"Is it?" Molly asks.

"It is. Do you think that I enjoyed missing our meeting? Do you think that I don't wish that the poker meeting fell under another day? I do. But Molly, I wouldn't miss the birth of our baby for my district."

Noah just did the worst thing you can do in the district business… tell a muggle that you're in the district business.

"District? What district?"

Noah briefly panics in his mind. He came up with an explanation. "The Russo Santino District. It's what restaurant owners call their restaurants, and it's kind of weird."

"That's beside the point," Molly says, without knowing she just saved Noah from a heart attack. "I'm worried that you aren't in it to win it with this family. You can't tolerate my father, my brother can't tolerate you, and now you might not be there for me when I need you."

Noah gives her a friendly embrace and kindly plays with her hair. "Molly, you are the love of my life. I wouldn't trade you or Ray for anything. I'm sorry that I hit you. I was in a crazy state of mind, and I wasn't thinking straight. I was terrible to you. I don't deserve you. I don't."

"Don't say that. Of course, you do. But Noah, I'm starting to see a pattern of your behavior. But, there's one thing I can't grasp."

"Is it why I've been acting weird lately? It's because I'm scared of being a father, and I don't think I'll perform as well as our baby deserves."

"No, it's not that. Why did you punch the mirror?"

Noah sighs, not wanting to answer the question. "Can I answer that question later? I have something for you."

"What do you mean?" Molly asks.

Noah smiles and puts his hand on Molly's face. "I was just going to get you flowers, but after what you've been through and what I've put you through, you deserve way more than daisies. I don't want you to think that this is me buying your love; this is me showing my appreciation of my lovely wife."

Noah reaches into his pocket and takes out a rectangular case. He hands it to Molly and says, "I love you, Molly."

Molly opens the box and sees the shiny necklace. Her jaw drops at the sight of the expensive gift. "Noah, you shouldn't have done this."

"No, don't say that. I should've done this a long time ago. This is long overdue, and I owe you the world."

She kisses him and wraps her arms around his neck. Noah wraps his arms around her waist. "We can't do this. Not right now; I have to see my therapist. Oh, and that reminds me. This hostess called for you, and apparently, some busboy dropped coffee on a kid."

"Jesus Christ, it was probably that Anthony kid. We need more busboys like Eric."

"Well, we'll reconvene later tonight," Molly says as she gives him one last kiss. "I'll give you a proper thank you later tonight."

"No thank-you's are in order. This was my thank you to you." Noah insists.

Noah enters the restaurant at around 5:00 PM wearing the same green unbuttoned shirt. He goes up to Henrietta and asks, "Where are the guys?"

"The private room. I wish you would've called so I could've given the guys notice."

"Hey, do you have a cigarette and a lighter?"

She hands him a lighter and says, "I thought you were more of a cigar guy?"

"I recently switched. What kind of cigs do you get?"

"Virginia Slims. Is that ok?"

"Yeah, I'm not picky," Noah responds.

Henrietta hands him a box of Virginia Slims and says, "Just take the box for now. Don't smoke until you get into the private room."

"Thanks. But why is it a full house? I thought that we would've shut down early due to the circumstances."

"Marco and Leo agreed that it's best to act as if nothing happened. We got the indication on the severity of the burn."

"Oh yeah? What is it?"

"Second degree. It burned about eleven percent of his body. Go in the room; they'll sort it all out."

"Ok, thanks."

Noah walks down the restaurant and smiles at all of the customers. He looks too informal to be running a nice restaurant, and most owners wear suits, not white tank tops and unbuttoned green shirts.

He enters the private room to see a man on a typewriter next to his brother and Marco. He shuts the door and says, "How bad is a second degree?"

"Better than third, worse than first," Leo says.

"No fucking shit. How much are we looking at money-wise?" Noah asks as he takes out a cigarette from Henrietta's box.

"Well, the medical bills aren't confirmed, but I predict at least three to four thousand dollars," Ian says.

"Who is this?"

"I am Ian Kyles; I'm your lawyer. We've met before, many times." Ian says as he offers his hand for a friendly handshake.

"Oh shit, my apologies. I don't recollect."

"No worries, I tend to be a pretty forgetful guy. Please, take a seat."

Noah sits down and lights his cigarette. "We think that the best thing for us to do right now is to enact this settlement as soon as possible."

"Well, that's a given. How much money are we talking about?" Noah asks as he lets out a gross puff of cigarette smoke.

"Well, it's always important to list a lower amount and let it be known that there is room for negotiation. Our starting point is eight thousand dollars."

Noah's jaw hits the floor after hearing that figure. It makes him want to clip Eric even more. "You know who should pay for this? Eric. Not us."

"Eric can't afford it, and he's a good kid. He made a terrible mistake, but the past is in the past. And this figure is quite hefty; we understand that. But I'm not going to let that Doner ad go to waste. If the settlement costs eight thousand, we're paying eight thousand. That's that. If you want to put it to a vote, be my guest. Besides, what do you want so desperately that you can't wait a month or two to purchase?"

Noah sighs; he knows that the news he's about to deliver isn't going to be taken smoothly. "Molly and I got into a fight."

Leo knows that something terrible is about to be presented to the already bad situation. "Noah, what the fuck did you do?"

"It's not that bad, ok? I just bought her some jewelry, that's all." Noah says.

"How much money did you spend?"

"Around two thousand. How the fuck was I supposed to know that Eric was going to spill coffee all over a kid? Besides, we are well aware of the fact that I can afford it."

Ian interjects, "Noah Santino, district head, can afford it without a doubt. But Noah Santino, co-owner of a steakhouse, can't afford to splurge on luxuries at a time of mild recession."

"This is just perfect; this is exactly what we needed. Do you know how many eyes are going to be on us? During times of mild recession, Noah Santino purchases jewelry! We are already set back enough, and let's not forget about the taxes on this settlement! Ian, how much do they tax on settlements?"

"Taxes are irrelevant in our case," Ian says.

"I thought settlements were taxable," Marco replies.

"The IRS taxes settlements since it comes out of your own pocket. Income tax. However, this is considered a personal injury settlement, which is nontaxable in the state of New York. What I'm more concerned about is the alibi. Money is tight, and Noah somehow can afford expensive jewelry. That doesn't look good."

"This isn't a fucking fashion show, and I don't give a fuck about what looks good or doesn't. If the IRS or any other government agency has a problem with me, they can come down here and kiss my fucking ass."

"You're a real comic. Let's stop wasting time on this IRS malarkey; there's a simple solution. Noah, you will have to return the jewelry. Simple!"

Noah laughs; he understands precisely what thoughts are running through his brother's head: *he'll do what I say, he won't argue, I own this kid, what a pushover he is, what a fucking sissy.* But Noah's thoughts differ just a tad bit: *you can't take this shit, Molly would freak, Leo doesn't own you...*and that's when he comes to the ultimate realization...*LEO DOESN'T OWN YOU. YOU ARE YOUR OWN MAN. LEO DOESN'T OWN YOU! LEO DOESN'T OWN YOU! DON'T TAKE THIS SHIT!*

Noah says to Leo, "Do you really think that's going to work?"

"It should. Is there a return policy we can refer to?" Leo asks.

"No, I'm not returning shit," Noah shouts. "Molly and I got into a terrible fight, and that's why I got it for her in the first place. For me to take it away...it would be despicable."

"Could you keep your voice down?" Marco demands.

"Despicable? What business do you think we are in?" Leo asks aggressively.

"It would be a different kind of despicable. You'll know the difference when you fall in love."

"You call that being in love? Having affairs isn't love. When you were fucking that hooker, did the state of despicability matter? No. That's why it doesn't matter here, either. You'll tell her that she'll get it when our financial stability is recovered."

Noah loses all of the screws in his head and goes berserk. "You know what? I'm not your fucking pushover Noah that you've known for all of these years! I'm not that Noah that'll just do as told! I'm not that Noah who takes this shit from lesser people! I am Noah-fucking-Santino! I'm a new man, and I don't put up with this shit anymore! If you want to pursue this settlement, then do it on your own!"

In bed at 8:43 PM, Noah watches *Magnificent Massacres* as he holds his wife. Molly is still tense from the mirror incident, and she's not mad or sad about what happened; she's severely curious about why it happened.

She watches her husband as he watches his program. *What would cause him to punch the mirror?*

"Honey, can I ask you something?" Molly asks, contemplating how to ask without making him go berserk.

"Sure."

Molly sighs, knowing there is no good way to ask why he clocked the mirror. She knows she can't let it go, no matter what he does or says. "Why did you punch the mirror?"

Noah gets up from the bed and shouts, "This shit again? Give it a rest! We aren't talking about it right now."

"You said we'll talk about it later."

"And we will!"

"It is later! This is important. This is very upsetting to you. Do you want me to bring you to my therapist?"

"Molly, leave it alone! I'll say this once and just once, ok? I saw Raymond! I saw him, and he was taunting me! I punched what I thought was him, but it was just a mirror. That's all it ever was. There!"

"Noah, I'm so sorry. Has this ever happened before?"

"I told you to leave it alone!"

"Noah, this is serious. It sounds like you are having hallucinations. I'd like for you to see my therapist. Mrs. Sheldon would love to meet with you."

Noah looks at his wife and just wants to chuck her off the balcony as Leo did to Raymond. He sincerely feels like his head is going to blow up.

"Shut your fucking yapper! All you do is make me want to blow my fucking brains out! I don't know what it is! I don't know if you're hormonal or just an uptight bitch, but you ought to hold back from acting like you run this place! I run this place!" Noah shouts.

Normally, Molly would get up and fight back. Normally, Molly wouldn't take this type of behavior from Noah. Normally, she would kick him out of the house or at least give a good old lecture. But, all she's capable of doing now is just cry…and that's what she does. Molly starts crying at the sight of her husband. She's not upset with him; she's worried for him.

Noah looks at his crying wife, and to his surprise, he doesn't feel bad for her. After Noah does some uncalled-for acts, he instantly goes to a state of sympathy for his poor wife. He looks at her and almost wants to feel bad for her, but he just doesn't.

"I'm going to go. I'll call in the morning." Molly says as he gets out of the bed.

"Molly, get back in the bed," Noah asks, but Molly proceeds to slip on her coat. "Molly, please get back in the bed!"

Molly puts on her slippers one by one and then grabs her purse. "Get rest, Noah."

Noah grabs Molly by her arm and says, "Molly, please! Get back in the bed!"

"I'm going out for an undetermined amount of time. I'll call you in the morning."

"Like hell you are. Do you know how late it is? It's nothing but rape and crime out in the mean streets. Get in bed!"

"I'm not your servant."

"Yeah, but you are my wife," Noah barks. "It's my sole responsibility to protect you."

"Is it your sole responsibility to backhand your wife when she's trying to help you?"

"Oh my fucking God, it was a reflex! You were disobeying me, and it was the heat of the moment!"

"I wasn't disobeying you; I was helping you. I was doing what any loving wife would do. I'm leaving! I don't care about what you say or do; I'm leaving. I feel more in danger in your presence than in the mean streets at midnight. I'll call you tomorrow."

"Molly, get in bed!"

"Or what? Are you going to backhand me?" Molly asks, slightly fracturing Noah's pride.

Noah knows that he can't reply or argue; it's done. Not the marriage, but the argument. However, Noah knows that marriage might be the next thing that goes down the drain.

Noah, without saying a word, just nods and wipes the tear-off of his face. Noah doesn't feel like this is a moment of clarity but a moment of defeat. His stress levels are through the roof, but he doesn't have enough energy to express himself to his wife.

Before Molly exits, she stops and just sighs for a moment. She puts both of her hands behind her neck and carefully takes off the expensive necklace. She places it in Noah's right hand and then puts his left hand on top of the jewelry. She looks her husband in the eyes and says, "I refuse to be pleased by anything other than your sincere apology. I looked at the jewelry brochure; you can still return it."

After Molly wishes for Noah to return the necklace, he feels like a failure. Not because his wife isn't happy with him, but because Leo and Marco now think he's not a team player. The fact that Noah wasn't willing to cooperate with the recession shows how minimal his dedication is to the alibi and the entire business.

"Molly, you don't understand how important it is for me that you keep this necklace."

Molly wipes the tears off of Noah's face and says, "Whatever has gotten into you…I pray that it gets out before this baby does."

CHAPTER 8:

ENTER SINFUL AND DYING

We don't normally recognize our inner workings,
but they work constantly.

The morning after the settlement enactment, Noah wakes up in his bed feeling drowsy and empty…mainly drowsy. Noah doesn't know where Molly is, he doesn't even know if she's alive.

The empty bottle of booze on the nightstand stares at its victim as he takes out a box of Callen cigarettes and a lighter. The bottle of alcohol has successfully diminished the very minimal amount of self-confidence that was holding Noah up.

As Noah lights his cigarette, deep feelings of fear and uncertainty start hitting him harder than a punch by Cassius Clay. *Is she ok? She said she'd call in the morning; why hasn't she called? Is she having an affair? Who would want to have an affair with a woman that has a massive lump on her stomach? What if she goes into early labor? What if she's in Philadelphia talking about how terrible I am to her father?*

Negative thoughts are starting to obtain Noah's sense of reality, and due to the substantial amount of recreational drugs he did the other night, they begin to turn it into a false one. Instead of reacting to whatever is leftover from last night's high from cocaine, he responds to the feeling of discomfort.

Noah isn't necessarily freaking out about his wife; he's more worried for himself. He's worried for his wife in the sense that if she dies, it will almost be like the blood will be in his hands…that's just one aspect of Noah's worries. Another factor would be how if Molly were to come back wanting a divorce, he'd lose his son. Noah still loves Molly, but he doesn't love her as he should.

The only thing Noah remembers from the previous night is drawing two lines next to the empty bottle of booze. He also remembers how terrible he felt when Molly left, but that's about all he can recollect.

At about 12:17 PM, Noah hears a loud ring from his nightstand phone. Do I pick up, or do I not? Noah's bones feel so weak, but then he realizes that it could be Molly. She said that she'd call. Noah picks up the phone and asks, "Molly?"

Colombo, who is on the other line, laughs and says, "Do I sound like Molly?"

Noah sighs in disappointment and says, "Oh, hey Jimmy. What's going on?"

"You tell me…you called me last night saying that you're out." Colombo barks.

"Oh, right. I ran out last night. Can I stop by the club later today?" Noah asks.

"Jesus Christ, you sound terrible. What the fuck happened to you?"

"Molly left."

"Who the fuck is Molly?"

"My wife."

"Oh, I'm sorry. When you say she left, do you mean divorce?"

"No, but that's not looking like an impossibility. It's getting a little bit rocky. She took off last night, and I have no clue where she is. She said she'll call in the morning, but I guess not."

"Ride it out; I'm sure it'll happen," Colombo assures. "Maybe swing by at around one or so."

"Sounds good."

After Noah hangs up, he feels his stomach rumble like never before. Is it the coke?

Noah goes downstairs and pours himself a bowl of cereal, which is only in his cabinet because Molly has cravings for sugary cereal from time to time. After he eats his cereal, his stomach is still empty. Jesus Christ, what the fuck is up with my stomach?

He cooks four turkey sausage links on the stove as he watches the morning news from the living room.

A handsome man named Morgan Stokes sits behind a desk with a gray suit and a piping hot cup of coffee on the news and says, "Welcome back. I am Morgan Carter. Actor Ronald Reagan has officially announced his candidacy for President. I don't see how or why an actor would think he could be the Commander in Chief, but we'll just have to wait and see."

After Noah finishes eating his links, he still feels hungry. He checks the freezer, fridge, cabinet, pantry…only ingredients. *Shit, I don't know how to make any of this.* Noah checks the time, 12:45 PM, and figures that he might as well get brunch at Bambino's. It sure as hell beats waiting for a phone call.

Noah enters the diner and goes up to the hostess stand. "Just one, please," Noah says.

The hostess grabs a menu and walks Noah to an empty table. Noah looks out of the window and thinks, *what if something happened to her?* Before he can contemplate anything, Mrs. Bambino approaches Noah.

"Hey honey, I haven't seen you in a while. How come you're not sitting with your brother?"

"Was he here earlier?" Noah asks.

"He's here right now with what looks like his girlfriend," Mrs. Bambino says as he points to a table with Leo and Henrietta splitting a chocolate milkshake.

"Oh, I had no idea. I'm going to go over and say hi." Noah says.

At the table, Leo is telling Henrietta one of his charming stories. After the settlement was concluded the night before, Leo offered to take Marco and Henrietta out for celebratory drinks. Henrietta went; Marco didn't. They went out, got drunk, woke up together, and decided to go out for brunch.

Noah approaches the table and sees his brother and his hostess laughing it up.

"Hey guys," Noah says, catching his brother off guard.

"Noah? What are you doing here?"

"Look, can I have a quick word with you?"

Leo sighs and says to Henrietta, "I'll be right back. Don't finish the milkshake without me."

Henrietta smiles at Leo's charm as he gets up from the table and walks with his brother to the other side of the diner.

"What's going on? I'm not very happy with you, and neither is Marco." Leo asks.

"I apologize for my behavior. I shouldn't have snapped at you like that, and I'm sorry if I hurt your feelings."

"Hurt my feelings? Noah, I have bones of steel; I don't care about what you said to me."

"Then what's wrong?"

"Isn't it obvious? Noah, we are still fresh, and you are showing the other district heads that you aren't very reliable. First off, you missed the apology meeting because you were fucking that hooker. Secondly, you wronged Abruzzo."

"Abruzzo is irrelevant; he's not an official district head. He's independent, remember?"

"Yes, but our partnership wants to acquire Abruzzo. We aren't going to acquire him if you mess shit up. That's why we had to do him that favor. But, let's move on from that…you have developed a pattern of being an unreliable leader. And yesterday, when you wouldn't comply with the settlement, it showed Marco how little you care about the restaurant." Leo explains,

"Wouldn't it look better for me to care more about the business than the restaurant?"

"The restaurant is a part of the business. I'm tired of hearing these excuses."

"Well, Molly left me last night. We got into a fight."

"About what?" Leo asks.

"Well, it all started when I hit her. Which I know sounds terrible, but it was in the heat of the moment."

Leo's jaw drops as soon as he hears that his brother hit his wife. "Noah, do us both a huge fucking favor. Never repeat that to anybody else. If you tell another district head about how you hit your wife…their respect will disappear faster than fire burns."

Any disrespect towards your wife or another head's wife is considered a sin. In the district business and the mafia, there are sins. If committed, these sins will not put you in any physical danger. However, other district heads will lose respect, which is terrible to lose in this racket.

"So you're telling me that these fuckers can sleep around and have girlfriends, and I can't lay some skin on my wife?" Noah asks.

"Do you hear yourself when you talk? Watch yourself; you already look bad to Marco. Which, by the way, you need to chip in your cut of the settlement."

"Ok, I will. Can we stop talking about business and start talking about how you are eating brunch with Henrietta? What happened to Mario's niece?"

"Red flag. She runs this restaurant, and boy does she love the fuck out of this place. I couldn't maintain a minute-long conversation with that chick without it leading to the restaurant. What are some of your hobbies? Running the restaurant. You have a sister, how old is she? Well, I opened my restaurant when she turned twenty-four, and I've had the restaurant for three years…so twenty-seven. Where were you when JFK was assassinated? The restaurant."

Noah laughs at Leo's story, and the district heads go back to being brothers. Noah continues to laugh and then asks, "So, how did Henrietta happen?"

"Well, we went out and got drunk to celebrate the settlement. Not a big story."

"So are you two just shacking up, or is this a real deal?"

Leo isn't what you would call a lady killer. With good looks and an Italian accent, Leo had all the girls in high school wanting him, but he didn't want any of them. Back then, he had his mind on other matters…kissing Raymond's ass.

But now, his brother is married and has a baby on the way; he wants to start his own Santino legacy. When Maria didn't work out, he promised himself that he'd reel in the next fish that grabs the hook.

"To me, this could be a real thing," Leo says happily. "We haven't talked about it, but waking up next to her was amazing."

"Is she aware of our real situation?"

"She's Marco's niece; of course, she knows about our situation," Leo explains.

"Huh, no kidding," Noah says. "I didn't know that they were related."

"How did you not know they were related? They have the same last name."

"Russo is a very common last name. Anyway, I'm happy for you. Meanwhile, my wife might be dead, and I have no way of contacting her, and I fucked up badly; she might file for divorce."

"Divorce? Are you out of your mind? What is she going to do? She's a housewife, for crying out loud, and she won't get a nickel, and she knows that. Do you really think she will go back to Philadelphia so she can live with her mid-class family? Do you think that she's willing to go from riches to rags just because you hit her? No!"

"Ok, but the love is slowly getting extinguished. I don't want my son to grow up with passionless parents as we did. I've decided not to have that affair."

"Wow. Heaven's gates are patiently waiting for your arrival now." Leo says jokingly.

The two brothers laugh. Leo says, "I have to go back to my date, but call me when Molly returns. Notice how I didn't say if, but when."

The brothers hug, and Leo returns to his little brunch date, and Noah goes back to his table and goes back to sorrow.

At 1:08 PM, Noah's cab arrives at Colombo's club. Noah has around seventy dollars in cash in his left coat pocket. In his right pocket, he has a box of Callen cigarettes along with a lighter.

He enters the empty club and sees Colombo behind the bar switching his Sears Sanyo television set. Noah shouts from across the empty club, "Hey Jimmy. What's going on?"

"I'm trying to find a decent program, any suggestions?" Colombo asks.

"Normally, I watch Magnificent Massacres, but that's not on until later. I normally just watch the news at this time."

"Eh, fuck it," Colombo says as he turns it off. "What amount are we going for this time?"

"Same amount."

Colombo reaches under the bar and picks up a locked briefcase. He puts in the combination and opens it up. "Ah, you're in luck. I have exactly that amount leftover from last night. Boy, oh boy, you should've been here last night. Chicks were off of the hook. We sold so much blow, it was great."

"You just sell blow to random strangers? What if they are undercover?" Noah asks.

"Smart thinking, but I'm way ahead of you," Colombo says with a smile. "Even when a cop is undercover, they are not allowed to take recreational drugs unless it's life-threatening. So, before we finish the transaction, we make them do a bump right before us for verification. Just safety measures. Enough about precautions; it'll be seventy dollars for the coke."

"Seventy dollars? Last time it was fifty."

"I thought that last time would be the last time. Fifty dollars was a friendly price, and I was happy to do it for you because I thought it was just for a special occasion. But something tells me that this won't be the last time you're buying from me. I'm sorry, but if I keep selling to you with friendly prices, I'll be breaking even instead of making a profit. It's seventy or nada."

"Seventy is all I have on me. I need to pay for a cab to go home. Could you cut it down to like sixty or sixty-five?"

"Sure. I can cut the cost down as much as you want, but then I'll have to cut the amount down. If I were you, I'd cut down by ten bucks and get a smaller amount."

Noah sighs and slaps the seventy bucks on the counter. "I'll walk."

Colombo looks at his vulnerable friend, so desperate for cocaine that he's willing to take a five-mile walk home so that he can have just a little more. Colombo hates to see his friend rot. "How about you take a week off of the coke? We'll see how you feel at the end of the week."

Noah feels like Colombo just locked him into a cocaine-free jail cell. How the fuck am I supposed to make it through the day without any lines?

"Jimmy, it's fine. Just give me the coke, and I'll be on my way."

Colombo sighs and knows that he can never refuse a transaction. It's not a sin or a rule, but it's his principle. He asks himself, why are you doing this to him, Jimmy? He grabs the money and slips it into the briefcase. Colombo asks Noah one last time, "Do you not see what is happening to you?"

Noah smiles and says, "Of course I do. I'm getting powerful, which has never happened to me before. The old me could never swat a fly; the new me can hit anyone. Even my wife, which I'm not very proud of, but I love the hints of progress."

"No, you're not getting powerful; you're getting carried away. You hit your damn wife. Who knows what else you could do?"

"Jimmy. Let me tell you something."

Colombo interrupts Noah, who he is not very fond of, to say, "Ay, you can forget about that Jimmy shit. It's Colombo to you from here on out. Do you understand me?"

"Jesus Christ, what's the matter with you? I thought we were friends." Noah says.

"I don't like those who hit wives. You can sleep around, you can make fun of her to your inner circle, but don't lay skin on her. This cocaine is turning you into an ass."

"You snort, too."

"Yes, but I don't let the white stuff control me," Colombo says as he hands him the bag of cocaine. "From now on, you only come to me for business. You can find somebody else that'll deal cocaine because I'm not going to promote your actions."

Noah's walk home is a long one: five miles, to be exact. All he does is think about how much everything is changing. In the past year: his wife got pregnant, his father got killed by his brother, his co-workers despise him, and he is addicted to cocaine.

He sees a homeless man sleeping on the side of the road. Usually, he would stop to check if he was ok and give him a helping hand. But all he does is continue walking down the street. Noah feels a part of him wanting to assist the homeless man, but that part of him is dying.

That part of him is trying to escape the cell that the cocaine put him in, but he can't. With cell bars made out of cocaine, he feels weak just grabbing them. Although he can't escape the jail, he shouts in an attempt to get Noah's attention. The dying part of him screams, "Go help him! Give him your cigarettes, at least!"

Noah stops walking for a moment; it's almost as if his legs aren't giving him a choice. He looks back at the homeless man who is sleeping vertically up against a blue mail bin.

The other part of Noah is made out of cocaine and the vault of his sins that he refuses to confess to a priest, even though he's a Catholic. This sinful part of him is the one holding the keys to the dying part. "Are you joking? Do you really want to give that guy cigarettes? What are you getting out of it?"

The dying part of him screams, "The feeling of doing something right, which we haven't had ever since you showed up."

"Hey, now don't you start accusing me of anything," the sinful part of him yells. "With you around, he's been nothing but a pushover. Everybody tells him what's what, and you let him comply. That foolishness has discontinued, and progress has been made. Do you want to go back to square one?"

"If square one was making Molly happy, waiting for his child to come out, and not worrying about a divorce: yes, I'd like to go back to square one."

Noah is now facing a crossroads: either appeasing the sinful part or appeasing the dying part. Noah doesn't know which way to go. At this moment, he's just a Manhattan native who's lost.

"Molly isn't going to leave him. Like Leo said, where would she go? What would she do? Go to Philadelphia and live with that loser father of hers? Also, this debate is unnecessary. If you want to help out a homeless man, why cigarettes? According to the medical reports, they aren't helping out much."

"Oh, you want to talk about medical reports? Do the medical reports mention anything about cocaine, you jackass?"

Noah takes out the cigarettes from his pocket and grasps them. Sinful says, "Ay, don't call me a jackass! Don't let him give him the cigs! We just spent seventy bucks."

"If we can spare seventy bucks for cocaine, we can spare a box of cigs," Dying says.

"Well, it doesn't matter. I'm bigger and stronger than you, and don't you even think for a second that he's taking anything you say to heart."

"The person you're turning him into is the person who Molly walked out on. If he wants a revelation, he needs to act fast." Dying proposes.

"A revelation? He already has had a revelation. He's hit new grounds. He doesn't let everybody push him around anymore. He doesn't need your input; he has me now."

Noah feels like the North Pole and looks at the homeless man as the South Pole. Noah feels drawn to the impoverished man who is in profound and, most likely, uncomfortable slumber. He looks down at his cigarettes and then back at the man. *What good are these at this point?*

He walks up to the homeless man and takes the lighter out of his pocket. "Why are you doing this? Just go home!" Sinful shouts.

Noah kneels on the hard cement ground and wonders how he should wake up the man. *Do I shake him or tap him?*

Dying says, "C'mon, just shake him."

Noah gently shakes the man back into consciousness. The old homeless man rubs his eyes and then notices Noah right in front of him. "You bastard! I had a good dream."

"I'm sorry, sir. I just wanted to know if you'd like to have these cigarettes, and it's either that or I throw them away."

The homeless man asks, "That's very thoughtful, but what kind of cigarettes?"

"What kind of homeless man is this guy? I've never seen such a picky homeless man." Sinful points out.

"Callen. Is that any good?"

"When you're on the streets, anything free besides Gilligane is good. Thank you very much. You wouldn't happen to have a lighter, would you?"

Noah places his lighter right next to the homeless man's legs. "That should do the trick."

Noah stands up and leaves the homeless man speechless and euphoric. The homeless man shouts, "Hey! You're a good man! God bless you."

Noah turns back and smiles at the homeless man without saying anything. Before Noah walks away, the man says, "Don't change."

Sinful turns silent, and Dying turns stronger. He still isn't strong enough to outweigh Sinful, but he's strong enough to put his hands on the cell bars.

Noah walks away from the homeless man feeling more satisfied than he's ever been with cocaine. However, cocaine doesn't necessarily satisfy him but enhances his mindset instead.

Four miles later, he gets to his house and opens up the door. In the dust room, where they put their shoes and coats, he notices that Molly's shoes are next to his. *Is she back?*

Noah hollers loudly, "Molly! Are you back, honey? It's me!"

"In the living room!" Molly hollers back at him.

Noah's heart drops, and feels more blessed than ever at that moment. He feels the light of God shine on him for the first time in eight months. Noah rushes into the living room to see his pregnant wife laying down on her back on the couch with her hands on her stomach.

"Honey, thank God," Noah cries. "I was so worried! Where have you been?"

"I stayed the night at a hotel. I would've called, but I was scared to hear your voice."

Noah gets closer to her head in an attempt to kiss her forehead, but she pushes him away. Not hard, but enough to get the point across. Noah looks at her confused; *why did she push me?*

"I'm still scared of you, Noah," Molly confesses. "Please sit on the chair beside the couch."

Noah nods and moves over to the chair. He sits down and smiles at his wife, who refuses to smile back. "Molly, I'm sorry. I'm not going to even bother with a whole spiel about how sorry I am because it's indescribable. I'll do whatever it takes. If therapy is what it takes, then it's therapy that I'll do. Whatever it takes, I'm serious about this."

Molly starts to cry again, and Noah genuinely can't tell whether it's hormones or genuine sadness. "Molly, please."

"I can't believe a word that you say. You've made me believe that you'll change, but all you do is get worse."

"This time is different. I'll do whatever it takes to prove it to you."

"Why is it different this time? What has changed?"

Noah sighs with delight and says, "On the way home, I spotted a homeless man asleep on the side of a mailbox. It felt like a part of me was telling me to walk away, but the other part wouldn't let me. I know it sounds crazy, but I was drawn to the man. I gave him my cigarettes and lighter, and it gave me a feeling of such happiness. It felt so nice to give, and then it made me feel even worse about you. I haven't given you anything but hard times and backhands. I'm sorry."

Molly nods along to her husband's excuse; it checks out for her. "I'd like for you to see my therapist."

"Fine by me. Whatever it takes."

"I'd like for you to sleep in the guest bedroom. I want my space from you for a bit, and I'm still a bit scared."

Noah smiles and asks, "Can I please hug you? If the answer is no, the answer is no. But I missed you so much, and I'd love to hug you."

Molly's tears drop on the couch after he asks that question. Noah smiles optimistically, hoping she'll abide. She wipes the tears off of her face and looks at her smiling husband, and says, "No.

Noah sighs, understanding why she wouldn't. But suddenly, to both of their surprises…Molly's water broke.

CHAPTER 9:

THE ABRUZZO DEAL

Sharks don't bite unless you make them.

P ete Abruzzo is a smart man. As the head of the only independent district, you have to prove your worth by doing undesirable things. For Abruzzo, he has to hide the truth from the mafia, districts, and pretty much everybody else.

When Pete was twenty-one, he took a massive loan from a loan shark to pay his mother's medical bills. If there's one thing about debt in New York is that they always catch up to you.

Currently, he has his riches stored in his brother's bunker in Chicago. Pete has a spending problem and knows that he will surely spend it quickly if he can access the money.

One afternoon, Pete reads the paper behind the counter in his donut shop and notices an article about Hugh Carey.

Governor Hugh Carey's Thoughts of the Upcoming Election.

Before he can read about how Carey is voting, three men in leather enter the shop: Aidan DeLoreto, Michael Buscemi, and Don Dylan. Aidan grabs the sign that displays "OPEN" and turns it to "CLOSED" without permission.

Pete notices the sketchy fellas messing with the signs. "Hey pal, put that sign back the way it was."

Aidan smiles and gives Pete a nice glare. He takes out a pack of Gilligane cigarettes and lights it up. Pete asks, "Is there something I can do for ya because you fellas are acting strange."

Aidan takes a nice puff from his cigarette and then snaps his fingers. Immediately, his crew takes out their pistols and points them right at Pete before he can even reach for a gun.

"Jesus Christ, what the fuck is this?" Pete asks.

"You owe my father a lot of money. Pay up, and we'll be on our way, alright?" Aidan says.

"I don't owe shit to nobody. If I were you, I'd lower those unloaded guns before I pull out the real deal." Pete threatens.

Aidan puffs on his cigarette and then says, "Mikey, put one in his foot."

Michael aims carefully and pulls the trigger while the gun is pointing towards Pete's foot. Blood splatters from Pete's foot and gets all over his nice pants. "Ahhh! You motherfuckers! My foot!"

Aidan smiles and pats Michael on the back. He lets out another nasty puff and then walks up to Pete, crawling all around the floor in terrible pain. Aidan puts his right foot on Pete's neck and says, "Is there anybody else in here? If you say yes, you will tell my boys where to find them. If you say no and we find out that you're lying, we'll not only kill them, but I will press my foot down, and I will press hard. Is there anybody else here?"

Pete, feeling unable to speak, shakes his head "no". Aidan nods and says, "Donny, scan the vicinity. Mikey, point your gun at this sad sack."

"You got it, boss," Donny says as he moves towards the back.

"Fellas! You've got the wrong guy! I just run a donut shop, that's it!" Pete claims.

"Ay, Abruzzo. If I were you, I'd shut your goddamn mouth unless you're going to tell us the truth. My father is Anthony DeLoreto. Ring a bell, you piece of shit?"

Pete abides and cries, "Fine! I took a loan from him a long time ago, and I can pay him back!"

"Well, now the price is forty thousand dollars. An extra five for each year you've left him hanging. It's to my understanding that my father just recently got in touch with you. You were scheduled to do a meet-up two nights ago, and he came back home without the money that is rightfully his, and now this is your final warning."

"I know what I did was wrong, but my wife got into a car accident in a cab. It's not my fault that I didn't make it."

"Yes, but it is your fault that you've left him dry for a few years. My father looked at you as a friend; you looked at him as a bank. As I said, this is your final warning. We will do a meet-up in the same spot at midnight. If we have to come back, you're a dead man. Do you understand?"

Pete, still holding onto his bleeding foot, says, "That won't work. My brother will have to come down here with the money, and that'll take a day at least. Could we do it tomorrow at midnight?"

"My father has had quite enough delays from you." Aidan insists.

Donny comes back from the back of the shop with his gun still out. "It's clear, boss."

"Donny, get this piece of shit back on his feet." Aidan orders as he puts out his cigarette in Pete's mug of piping hot coffee.

Donny grabs Pete from his shoulders and picks him up. Pete stands on the ground, but his foot is killing him. "Abruzzo, why don't you fetch me a dozen?"

Pete nods as tears of pain start to shed. He hops over to the stack of folded-up dozen boxes and picks one up. He unfolds it back into the rect-angular box form and asks, "What do you want?"

"What kind of sprinkles are on top of your chocolate donuts?"

Pete stutters as he cries, "It depends on which kind you want. The regular is just rainbow sprinkles, but the double-time is chocolate sprinkles."

"The double-time is chocolate sprinkles on top of chocolate frosting? Hell yeah, that sounds good. Get me four of those double things. Mikey, what do you want?"

Mikey browses the selection of pastries and says, "Those bear claws look pretty fucking good. Get me four of those."

Pete finishes putting the chocolate donuts in and then starts with the bear claws. Donny spots a Boston cream and says, "Gimme four of those Boston creams."

Pete finishes putting in all of the donuts and then seals it properly. He hands the box to Aidan. He snags the box out of Pete's hand and says, "Thanks for the donuts. Sorry about the foot; I'd clean the blood off of these white floors if I were you. Anyway, be there tonight. No more excuses. I don't care if your wife has a stroke or your father gets slammed by a bus; if you're not there, then you're going to wish you were in one of those positions rather than the hell we'll put you through."

Aidan and his crew walk out of the donut shop, leaving Pete helpless and dying on the inside. He doesn't know where to go or what to do. Who the fuck has that kind of cash lying around? He can't get his brother down to Manhattan on such short notice; he only has money to spend on essentials, he can't take a loan from the mafia because they are ruthless, he can't take a loan from the districts because they'll never abide, he's lost. But then he realizes he has one resort left. What's the one thing that will get the districts on board? A partnership.

After a long and steamy night of drinking and more drinking, Leo is in a deep sleep with Henrietta sharing the sheets with him. Leo feels complete happiness with his left arm wrapped around her and her left palm flat on his chest. He doesn't want anything altered. But of course, something always goes wrong whenever everything feels right.

The phone on his coffee table starts to ring loudly. It wakes up Henrietta first, and then she wakes up Leo. He rubs his eyes and asks, "Why did you wake me up?"

"Do your ears not work? The phone is ringing."

Leo sighs and says to himself, "Fuck this, it's too early."

"Babe, it's almost ten. Russo Santino is serving brunch in fifteen minutes." Henrietta laughs as she pets Leo's hair.

Leo picks up the phone and asks, "This is Leo."

"Leo, I'm calling you from the Bellevue hospital. Molly's in labor! Come by now!" Noah exclaims.

"Jesus Christ, I'll get ready right away. How is she doing?" Leo asks.

"She's fine; just get here as soon as possible," Noah says as he hangs up.

Leo gets out of bed and rushes over to his closet. "What's going on? Who was that on the phone?"

"Noah's wife is in labor," Leo says as he takes off a shirt from a hanger. "I have to get dressed; I can't miss this."

"Should I get ready as well?" Henrietta asks.

"I would love it if you could join me. Do you have plans?" Leo asks as he buttons his shirt one by one.

"Nothing. I'm as free as that prostitute who sleeps on the sidewalk next to Russo Santino." Henrietta jokes.

Leo laughs and stares at his woman; he feels madly in love with her. For the first time in years, he feels love and not the kind of love you have because of your family. Henrietta is a beautiful woman, and Leo can't believe she's under his bedsheets.

As Leo slips on some pants, his phone starts to ring again. Leo asks Henrietta, "It's probably Noah. Could you answer it?"

Henrietta scoots over to the other side of the bed and answers, "This is Henrietta."

On the other line, a hurting Pete Abruzzo holds his phone and asks, "Is Leo Santino there?"

"Yes, who is this?"

"This is Pete Abruzzo. Tell him this is urgent and that he needs to answer right now." Pete barks.

Henrietta puts the phone to her shoulder and says, "Some guy named Pete Abruzzo is barking at me. He says it's urgent."

Leo rolls his eyes and says, "What does this prick want?"

Henrietta hands him the phone, and he snatches it angrily. He briefly sighs and then answers, "Hey Pete, you've caught me at a bad time. Noah's wife is in labor."

"That probably will make this a whole lot better; I've never been too fond of that brother of yours," Pete says. "I need you to come down to the donut shop. Don't ask any questions; they will all be answered at the shop."

"Pete, I can't attend. I have to go to the hospital for the birth of my nephew. Perhaps another time."

"This is a necessary meeting. Have you ever heard of those?" Pete asks, slickly referencing the district law of attending all district meetings regardless of the circumstances.

"Pete, don't call again. I'm sorry, but this isn't a debate. Goodbye, Pete." Leo says as he hangs up.

"What was that all about?" Henrietta asks as he puts her skirt back on.

"Beats me," Leo says. "Do you know where I might've put my watch? I get very fidgety when I don't have my necessary items with me."

"Is it not on the coffee table?"

"No, I would've seen it already."

"Is it on the bathroom counter?"

"I've been in here the whole time; how could I have checked?"

"Jesus, I was just trying to help. No need for that attitude."

"I'm sorry, baby. I'm sorry. As I said, I get stressed when I'm missing stuff." Leo insists.

The phone rings again, and Leo's head metaphorically explodes. "I swear to God if it's that Abruzzo riff-raff again, I'll shoot my goddamn phone."

Leo walks up the phone and answers, "Who is this?"

"It's Mario. I heard that Noah's wife is going into labor. Congrats on being an uncle. That's great, but Pete tells me that you aren't coming down to the shop. You and Noah must."

"Mario, I can't. And Noah can't either; his son is coming today."

"I understand how unfortunate the timing is, but unfortunately, this is a meeting. Do I need to remind you of your father's historic decision?"

When Mario says "historic decision", he is talking about how Raymond missed the birth of Leo and Noah to attend a meeting that would lead to the creation of Russo Santino. This is what made Raymond an organized crime legend, even amongst some mafia families.

"I'll be there. But I can't reach Noah. He's at the hospital."

"Which one?" Mario asks.

"The Bellevue or something like that. I'll be on my way, but he won't be, so don't expect him."

"Leo, this won't look good for your brother."

"It's out of my hands, Mario. What do you want me to do?"

In the hallway of the hospital floor that Molly is giving birth on, there is a long line of chairs that Molly's family and husband occupy. Noah sits next to Nathan and the rest of the family that took the first available flight to New York.

Maya loves Noah, but only because she has to because he's the father of her grandchild. Nathan hates Noah's guts, and the feeling is mutual. Adam hates his guts as well, but Noah doesn't know that. However, there is one fact that everybody in these chairs knows is true: they are dysfunctional in-laws.

With Nathan being a cop, Noah feels extra alert whenever he sees him. That's another major factor to why Noah doesn't like Nathan coming over, but now it's as if he has no choice. He already decided that it's time to make nice with his in-laws, and he's going to do so by hosting a barbecue at his house.

"So, Noah. How is the restaurant business going for you?"

"Oh, it's alright. We just had to sign a settlement because a busboy spilled coffee on a kid." Noah says.

Nathan chuckles and takes a sip of his coffee from his plastic cup, and then says, "Wow. It sounds like you have quite the staff over there, huh?"

Maya slaps Nathan's arm and says, "Oh, don't listen to him. He's just giving you a hard time, honey."

Noah smiles and stays silent, hoping she'll take the hint that he doesn't want to talk. Nathan whispers to Maya, "Did Molly ever tell you what she changed the name to?"

Noah overhears this and loses his marbles. "I'm sorry, what did you just say?"

"Well, I was just wondering what the baby's name was changed to."

"We didn't change the name, and we aren't going to." Noah snaps.

"Why not? Ray isn't a Jewish name."

"Well, Ray isn't a Jewish baby."

Nathan laughs again and says, "I beg to differ."

"You can beg all you want, but that's not changing the baby's religion," Noah says.

"You do realize that the religion is passed down through the mother, don't you?"

"Nathan, it's their son. I'm sure that they have an arrangement." Maya insists.

"Well, I'd love to hear it from Molly."

Leo pulls into the parking lot in between a deli and Pete's donut place. He takes the spot next to Mario's car, puts the car in park, and leaves the keys in the ignition. He takes out his wallet and says to Henrietta, "Hopefully, this won't take long. But, you never can tell with these guys."

"What's this meeting even about?" Henrietta asks.

"I don't know; they aren't able to tell us over the phone," Leo says as he hands her a couple of bucks. "Go get yourself a sub from the deli. I'll leave the keys with you."

"Alright, have a good meeting."

Leo kisses Henrietta and says, "Thanks for tagging along."

Leo opens the door and then shuts it as he makes his way to the sidewalk. He debates whether or not he should light a cigar, but he fears that it'll be an extremely brief meeting and he'll have wasted a high-quality cigar. He decides against it and just walks up to the door and sees that the sign says "CLOSED". Must be necessary, he thinks.

He sees through the glass door that Marco, Mario, and Robert are standing next to Pete, who sits down on a chair with his foot wrapped up. Leo walks in and asks, "What's up with your foot?"

"Fucking loan sharks! They have no mercy!" Pete barks.

"There's a saying my old man had: the shark with the hardest bite is always a loan shark," Leo says. "Why is Mr. Abruzzo getting mixed up with loan sharks?"

"I took from them when I was in Jersey. I was young in stupid, but that's beside the point."

"Then what is the point, Pete? The clock is ticking." Leo says.

"Leo, there are two rules with meetings that you have to cooperate with: attendance and patience," Mario says.

Leo snaps and grabs Mario by the lapel of his suit and says, "With all due respect, I'm potentially missing the birth of my brother's baby. I don't want to hear shit about cooperation, and I also don't want to hear shit about my father's historic decision. I'm not my father, and neither is my brother, so get that in your head."

Mario gives Leo a dirty look and says, "Get your hand off of my suit."

Leo, knowing he made a big mistake, nods and let's go. He fixes the messed-up lapel and says, "I'm sorry, you just have to understand that this is a very stressful situation."

Mario winks as his way of saying, don't worry about it. Leo and Mario are good friends; no fights last long, and that's the way it's supposed to be regardless of whether it's a friendship or just a partnership.

"I'll make this quick. I only have like four thousand dollars on me; my brother has it stored in his little bunker in Chicago. I have a spending problem, so it should be in my brother's bunker rather than Mario's storage. I need forty thousand by tonight, or else I'm a goner."

Marco laughs and asks, "Are you seriously asking us for a loan? You know the rules; we can only loan money within the group. You're independent, remember?"

"I'm not looking for a loan; I'm looking for a buyout. If you guys spare the sixty thousand dollars, I'll become a district in your group partnership."

Robert smiles, so does Leo. Pete is the only independent district that sets them back a bit more than preferred, so this sounds like the best deal to all of them. "I don't speak on behalf of my colleagues, but I'm in," Robert says.

"I don't see why not," Mario says.

In all honesty, Mario isn't gaining much from this deal. However, he understands that it's essential to the group as a whole.

"You bet your ass I'm in," Marco says.

Remember, Marco is in the shipment business. Leo and Noah will be saving money from the gun deals, which means a slightly bigger cut for Marco.

"I'm in, and Noah is too."

Colombo isn't at this meeting because he has a minimal role in the group, so will Pete after this deal. Since he's in narcotics, this deal is irrelevant to him because neither district will benefit from the other.

HOW THIS ARRANGEMENT WILL WORK WITH THE BRUNO DISTRICT: Robert gets a hit gig, and him and his crew need a specific type of firearm. Instead of renting or buying from Pete, they just borrow, and Pete gets a cut of the gig.

HOW THIS ARRANGEMENT WILL WORK WITH THE ALFREDO DISTRICT: Pete will continue to store his stuff with Mario, but he'll get the storage for less money. What does Mario gain? Not much.

HOW THIS ARRANGEMENT WILL WORK WITH BOTH THE BRUNO DISTRICT AND THE SANTINO DISTRICT: Leo and Noah are distribution, so that means they find somebody who needs firearms, and they take them from Pete without purchase. This means lower prices which means more clients. As always, Marco gets a cut and a much bigger one now that more money is earned, and Pete will get a cut.

None of the arrangements, besides Mario's, are ideal for Pete. However, when it comes to the point where it's less money or safety, you're going to want to pick safety.

"I did the math, and it'll be eight thousand from each of you," Pete says.

Leo says to Mario, "Alright, just take the eight from mine and Noah's."

"I'm sorry, I can't take money out of Noah's storage without his verbal consent," Mario says.

"Ok, no problem. I'll have him call you from the hospital."

"Are you fucking high?"

"It'll be in code. He'll call you up and say that it's him and that he agrees." Leo explains.

"No, that won't work. I need to hear him say the amount he consents to deposit in person."

"Why can't he just say it in code over the phone?"

"It's my father's rule."

"What is it with you and taking after fathers?" Leo asks.

"Watch your mouth! If he doesn't say it to me in person, I'm afraid I can't take it out."

"He can't leave the hospital; he could miss the birth of his baby. Could you come down?"

"I don't want to sound inconsiderate, but I already have enough on my plate."

"Leo, I think that you have to take out the money from your storage on his behalf. He'll pay you back." Pete says.

"Do you expect me to give up sixteen thousand dollars?"

Pete desperately says, "He'll pay you back immediately."

"What if he doesn't?" Leo asks.

"He doesn't have a choice," Marco says. "C'mon Leo, be a team player."

The sound of that amuses Leo. It would look really good if I were a team player, Leo thinks to himself. "Alright, take sixteen thousand out. Profits will be made over time, I suppose."

Henrietta is digging into her meatball sub as Leo enters the car. With her mouth full of beef and tomato sauce, she asks, "How did it go?"

"I hate Mario sometimes. I get it's his procedure, and it's a very smart one, but it's setting me back sixteen grand." Leo rants as he turns the car back on.

"Slow down; what's going on?" Henrietta asks as she swallows her bite of the sub.

"I'd rather not get into it right now," Leo says.

"Suit yourself," Henrietta says as she takes another bite.

"That sub smells good."

"It's a meatball sub. Do you want a bite?"

"No, it's messy food, and I'm a messy person. I'll get something to eat at the cafeteria in the hospital or something. We have to get a move on; my baby nephew could be born already."

Noah bites his fingernails as he sits next to his brother-in-law, talking to his father-in-law about his work, "So, I signed for two years. They asked me if I'd like to renew my contract, but I got a better offer."

"I don't see why you don't take the better offer."

"Because I'd have to start all over again. I'm comfortable with where I am in my company."

Adam is the only one in the family who knows about Noah's backhand incident. He wishes he could inform his father, but Molly swore him to secrecy.

Noah sinks and sinks more and more into his seat as he hears their dull dialogue exchanges. He feels himself fall asleep, which he knows would look bad. So he excuses himself and busts a move to the bathroom.

He locks the bathroom door and then whips out a little baggie of cocaine and takes out a snuff spoon (tiny spoons used to snort cocaine). He takes a little scoop of the cocaine and takes a sniff. Little by little, Noah wakes himself up the only way he knows how.

When he looks back into the mirror, he sees his father again. Raymond is lighting a Cuban as he stares at his weak son. "Boy, oh boy, Colombo has really done a number on you. Cocaine on the birth of your child?"

"At least I showed up to his birth instead of having some drinks," Noah replies with aggression.

"If it weren't for my historic decision, you would've grown up polishing shoes instead of having them polished for you. I'm not here to break your balls; that's what Nathan is for." Raymond says with a chuckle.

Noah ignores his arrogant father as he lets out a fat puff of cigar smoke. Raymond always conveys a despicable vibe, but now it feels more sinister to Noah. "Seriously, I sincerely thank you for naming your child after me.

I also applaud you for standing your ground in the whole religion debate. This white stuff is killing you, but at least you're growing a pair."

"Why do you keep appearing to me? Why can't you leave me alone for once?" Noah asks.

"How would I know? It's your hallucinations, you tell me." Raymond says, and then he disappears.

When Noah exits, he sees Leo and Henrietta talking to Nathan and Maya. He dashes over to his brother and gives him a warm embrace. "What took you so long?" Noah cries.

"I'll explain in just a moment. How is Molly?" Leo asks.

"She's alright. Just chewing on ice chips." Noah responds.

"How are you?"

"I'm losing my mind."

"Then you're probably not in the mood to talk business."

"Business, politics, whatever you want."

Leo says, "Let's step aside for a moment."

The brothers walk away from the waiting chairs, stand next to the water coolers, and act as if they are having a casual conversation while getting a drink of water.

"So, good news and bad news. The good news is that Abruzzo is joining the group partnership." Leo says.

This comes to Noah's surprise, but it puts him in a better state of mind. "That's terrific, and that's a breakthrough for us."

Leo scratches his head, knowing he has to serve this following announcement with caution of potential outcomes. He knows that Noah is very conservative when it comes to his green. However, Noah has pushed for this deal in the past, so Leo thinks that there is a chance that this won't lead to a famous Noah outburst.

"Look, you may not like everything about this situation, and to tell you the truth, neither am I. This isn't what we had in mind for this deal. It's steep."

"Steep? What do you mean?"

"Well, he owes a bunch of money to loan sharks. The stupid fuck thought that he could hide from them. Well, now he's desperate. He has all of his cash in Chicago, and he needs the money by tonight. In summary, each of us is down eight thousand." Leo explains.

"Eight thousand? You say that very casually, but that's not a simple thing to say. Jesus Christ, Mario took out my money without my consent?"

"No, on the contrary. He took out an additional eight from my storage because you weren't there to agree. You'll just have to reimburse me." Leo says.

"What? Are you out of your goddamn mind? So, I went down by three because of a coffee spill. Now I'm down eight?"

"This is a good thing; you wanted this to happen."

"I didn't want to be down eight grand for this! Jesus Christ, how much money does a man have to lose?"

"Would you relax? It's going to become profitable over time. Also, let's be real: if you don't pay up, it's not going to look very good for you. Do you just want me to cover you and be down sixteen grand?" Leo insists.

"I'm not coughing up, end of discussion. Maybe if you waited to take my vote, you wouldn't be down sixteen. I went with the recession because that was necessary. This Abruzzo deal isn't necessary to me. His partnership is not worth eight grand, and I'm mad that you made this decision on my behalf. From now on, converse with me before these deals."

"We were on a ticking time bomb; I didn't have time to converse with you. This deal is what's best for the group and best for our district, and that's a fact. I'll be expecting your share by the end of this week, and that's that." Leo orders.

"If you want him in, you pay the piper. I do not financially involve myself in this deal."

"You selfish prick! I'm tired of carrying the weight! Come on, Henrietta, let's get out of here!" Leo says.

"Oh, so now you're missing the birth of your nephew?" Noah barks with hostility.

Leo laughs and says, "You know what? You're right. That wouldn't be very fair of me to miss Ray's birth just because his father is an absolute asshole."

For the next hour, Leo and Henrietta chat amongst themselves on the chairs. Noah watches the couple giggle and talk, which makes him reminisce about that time of his relationship with Molly where that was natural.

Eventually, the doctor enters the main hallway and approaches Noah, who is slumped into his chair. "Mr. Santino, it's time."

As Noah gets up, Nathan and Maya get up with him. Nathan walks up to his son-in-law and gives him a handshake. "Give my daughter my best wishes."

Maya comes up to Noah to hug him and kiss him on the cheek. "The time has finally arrived."

Adam gives Noah a friendly handshake and a casual pat on the back, and they don't say anything to each other. As Adam sits down, Leo stands up, and he walks up to his brother and hugs him. Leo whispers into his brother's ear, "Let's hope this Ray turns out better than the last."

Noah and Leo laugh for a second, and then the brothers separate from the embrace and give each other a nod saying, it's ok. Noah smiles and then walks into the delivery room.

About an hour later, Noah and Molly share the hospital bed as they both hold their son. Noah is on the verge of tears; Molly has tears dropping on her baby's head. "He's so beautiful." Molly lets out.

"He looks like me when I was born. Have you seen my baby photos?" Noah asks.

"Please, that's all Sofia would show me. She would show me pictures of you and your brother in the tub, and she'd have me guess which one was you."

Noah takes comfort in hearing stories of his mother. He never really talks or even thinks of his mother, but that's mainly because his father dominates his terrible past.

As he looks at his son, he for once sees something that doesn't just belong to him. It's not just his baby; it's Molly's baby. He thinks about how Molly went through hell for nine months, and he realizes that he hasn't done anything to help her.

He also thinks about how much she loves her father and how much her father loves her. Noah's father wants the baby to be Catholic, but Molly wants the baby to be Jewish. As much as he hates to admit it, he knows that his wife and father-in-law deserve this baby more than he does. He comes to terms with the fact that his father hasn't done anything for him, so why appease him? He is aware that his father will continue to haunt him if he doesn't name the baby after him, but then he figures out that his father will continue to haunt him regardless.

"Do you like the name Ray?" Noah asks.

"Why do you ask?"

"Because I think that Ray isn't such a good name. Neither is Raymond. Maybe he's better off following your traditions. Look, I've been terrible. I know that. All I've done is work and make sacrifices for the wrong cause. You deserve this baby more than I do. If I get the religion, you get the name. It's only fair."

Molly smiles and grabs Noah's hand. As she holds it, she feels his love, and she knows it's genuine. This is all she wants: not jewelry, cars, cosmetic products, just his true love.

Noah isn't happy with everything about this situation, but it's no matter. If Molly's happy, he's happy. He still isn't the perfect husband; he still hides his old affairs and current cocaine addiction. However, after three months of being a cocaine addict: Noah is starting to turn around.

After Noah says all of this, Dying grasps the bar of his cell. Sinful may be holding the keys to the cell, but Dying is holding the bars. He sends a smile towards his adversary and says, "Looks like you're outweighed on this one."

"Oh, you can celebrate as much as you want. If I can't alter this now, I can surely alter this later when the opportunity presents itself." Sinful responds.

"If you are so capable of changing his mind, why don't you do it now while I'm still in this cell?"

"The timing isn't right. He just had a baby; I'll let him have this moment. Don't you dare even think for a second that you're bringing him back to the way he used to be."

"Well, I can spot progress."

"Where? When he went into the bathroom and snorted?"

"No, when he just declared that he'll sacrifice his wishes for this baby for Molly's," Dying says.

"Just shut your mouth, alright? Don't forget that I'm still stronger than you." Sinful snaps.

Dying grabs the bar and uses all of his strength to snap them off. He exits his cell and asks, "Says who?"

Sinful is no longer against Dying but against Healing.

CHAPTER 10:

SINCERELY, NOAH

Noah's out.

It's a week after the birth of Nathan Jr. Santino. Nathan is happy to see his son-in-law turn around and is delighted to have his grandson named after him.

Even though it's a happy ending for the Santinos and Hoffmans, many changes are left to be made. Noah has to scratch "Ray" out of all of the banners that say "Ray Santino" and replace it with "Nathan Jr.". Noah decides that he'll call his baby Junior; Molly is fine with that.

Noah has two coolers in his backyard: one with beers and one with sodas. In the living room, he has several buckets of potato chips and a bowl of fruit punch. He also has his liquor set up in the bar on the outside of his house. One of the bonuses of having a home in Ossining is that the backyards are spectacular.

Noah is grilling a few sausage links on top of the grill as he talks to his brother. "Do you think that I'm doing the right thing with this whole name thing?"

Leo is busy sipping on his bottle of Sprite and then says, "Noah, I ain't no shrink, but I think what you did shows a lot of growth. She needed something that would help her hang onto the relationship, and you gave it to her. Don't let any negative thoughts on the matter stay put."

Nathan spots Noah and Leo grilling. He starts to head over to the grill to break his son-in-law's balls; Noah notices and says, "Oh great, look who's coming over to us."

"Behave. You've done something very generous; what's he going to do?" Leo asks as he drops his bottle into the trash can.

Nathan comes over to the grill and looks at Noah cooking. "I have to say that I'm impressed, and I didn't know you could cook."

"I grill from time to time," Noah says.

"From time to time? Why not more often and give my daughter a break?" Nathan asks as he drinks from his bottle of Coors.

"Your daughter is a very gifted cook. I'm always out working; I don't have a lot of time to set up the grill every night." Noah explains.

"Well, a real barbecuer can grill anytime, anywhere," Nathan says.

"Then why don't you barbecue while I drink Coors and insult the man of the house. With all due respect, I know what I'm doing."

"Really? Well, if I were you, I'd lighten up and flip over that link." Nathan says as he makes his way to the interior of the house.

"Ok, you're right. He's a total asshole." Leo admits.

"Sometimes I hate him more than Raymond," Noah responds. "I have to take a leak. Could you watch the links for me?"

Noah snorts a line in the bathroom in an attempt to erase his encounter with Nathan. He snorts away his problems because his son shares the name of the man he hates the most. He snorts away the embarrassing moment when he praised his barbecuing skills to Nathan and then got called out for not flipping it over in time.

When he looks up from his sink, he stares into the mirror and sees Raymond once again. "Jesus Christ, at this point, you just want me to haunt you."

Noah ignores him and puts his baggie of cocaine back into his cigar box. "How could you allow such disgraceful names into the home that I purchased for you?"

"Pops, just drop it. I'm doing what's right for my wife, and I'd take notes if I were you."

Noah turns on the faucet and starts to wash his hands. "You can't even stand up to that Nathan fella. How fucking pathetic are you? All you do is snort cocaine and switch from mood to mood. I am proud of you for putting Leo in his place. Have you noticed how he's been so much friendlier lately?"

"That's not my accomplishment; it's Henrietta's. However, he only gets hard on me when it comes to the business that you pushed us into."

"That I pushed you into; are you serious? If it weren't for this business, you would be flipping patties at a diner during the graveyard shift."

"What a savior you are." Noah snaps sarcastically.

"Don't get smart with me. You're weak. Your brother wouldn't have backed down like a coward, and you should follow his example more often."

"Would you just shut the fuck up?" Noah snaps furiously.

Raymond laughs and asks, "What are you gonna do, hit me?"

After just a blink of Noah's eye, Raymond disappears. Noah is now in the bathroom alone, but it doesn't feel better. He feels like Raymond won that one.

Meanwhile, Mario and his wife, Mallory, pull into Noah's driveway. His father, Antonio, is asleep in the backseat with his two grandkids, Anthony and Arianna. "Could you grab the wine? I have to wake him up and get the kids out of their car seats." Mario asks.

"Sure thing," Mallory says as she goes to the backseat to grab the bottle of wine they just purchased.

Mario opens the back door and starts shaking his old father awake. Once he wakes up, he asks, "Jesus Christ, are we here already?"

"Yes, c'mon. You had a whole forty-five-minute drive to nap; it's time to wake up." Mario insists.

"My goodness, they have such a gorgeous home. I can't wait for you to retire so we can move here."

"What's wrong with Manhattan? You love Manhattan. Since when have you loved Ossining?" Mario asks as he helps his father up from the car.

"Yes, but I'd love a real house. I love our townhouse, but I want us to have a backyard one day for the kids to play in." Arianna says as she gets the kids out of their car seats.

"If anything, you two should move to Italy. What a place to live; I miss it over there." Antonio interjects.

"We're staying put. We don't need a glamorous life in Ossining. Imagine having to drive an hour just to get to your place of business." Mario insists.

"That's the whole point of retirement."

Leo is out in the backyard smoking an Old Port cigar with Adam, who is also puffing on one. "This country is going down the drain."

"I don't normally vote, but you better believe I'm voting this time around. I like Reagan; Noah and I used to watch his films when I was younger." Leo says.

"A couple of years ago, when I was at this other place, I had a great position in the workplace. I was in the big leagues. I got offered a job for less money at Doner but a higher position. Carter wanted to use us to run his campaign ads, and they put me in charge of the project. I refused, and I ended up leaving that higher paying job for Doner."

"That's what I respect. When a man stands up for what he believes in knowing he's not getting anything out of it except for pride."

Robert pulls into the driveway next to Mario's car with a knitted blanket that his wife, Gloria, made in the backseat. "This fucking prick has a whole fucking house in Ossining while we are stuck in that blob-of-crap townhouse."

"Be nice; he was nice enough to invite us to this after the fallout." Gloria insists.

"He invited me out of fear; I just know that he did," Robert says as he takes the knitted blanket out of the backseat. "He doesn't deserve this house; we deserve this house. I bust my ass, and for what?"

Noah is in the living room staring at the TV as he hears conversations from people, most of whom he doesn't care for, in the living room as they eat Noah's famous burgers.

Molly is with all of the wives, talking about how the delivery went, the baby's behaviors, and other parenting stuff. The other wives are drinking Noah's expensive wine, but Molly is sipping her coffee. Even though she can drink alcoholic beverages, she claims to have missed caffeine more than alcohol.

Noah looks over to the other side of the house, where he sees his brother talking to his brother-in-law. He sees them laughing and drinking while he's sitting and frowning. He watches Adam and Leo get along, and this makes him highly insecure.

Noah turns his head to the left and directs his attention to the spectacle of Nathan having a friendly chat with Marco. Nathan is eating one of the hot dogs Noah made, and so does Marco.

Noah looks back at the TV and sees the headline.

Little Richard retires for religious pursuits.

Noah nods at the headline and takes a sip of his beer. He sets the bottle back on the counter and then spots Marco heading right his way. *Oh great, now I have to deal with hearing him talk about how swell Nathan is,* Noah thinks to himself.

Marco sits on the couch next to him and says, "I just finished talking with your pops."

"He ain't my pops," Noah says.

"Your wife's, whatever the case. You could've given us a warning about him."

"A warning about how big of a prick he is?" Noah snaps as he finishes his beer.

"He's a fucking cop, Noah. I should've been aware of this." Marco says.

"Did you say anything about our arrangement?" Noah asks.

"No, I'm not fucking stupid. I don't like talking to blue boys, and I wouldn't have approached him if I knew."

"Well, now you do. Don't talk to him anymore if you don't want to, ok?"

Marco thinks to himself, this prick has been cruisin' for a bruisin', and he's arriving at his destination.

Marco sighs and says, "Where is your bathroom?"

Noah points to the bathroom, and then Marco gets up from the couch, leaving Noah empty once again.

Marco washes his hands thoroughly with this nice smelling soap that Molly likes to purchase in the bathroom. He smells his hands and thinks, *this is pretty good quality soap.* He washes his hands more and thinks, *I wonder what other premium shit this asshole carries.*

He opens the cupboard above the sink and sees toothpaste, bagged hand soap, more toothpaste, and a cigar box of Glens. I haven't puffed one of those in a while.

Marco picks up the box and notices that the weight distribution of the box isn't very proportionate. It's too light for a box of cigars, Marco thinks.

He slowly and carefully opens up the box to check out what this is all about, and then he sees Noah's bag of cocaine. *No fucking way this pussy is snorting.*

Marco doubts that it's actually cocaine, but maybe just baby powder or some other possible substitute. He dips his pinky into the cocaine and brings it back up to his nose. He closes his eyes and snorts, making his eyes pop wide open.

"Motherfucker!" Marco shouts as he shoves the box into his back pocket.

Colombo's taxi pulls up to the side of the house. From Manhattan to Ossining, cab fare is pretty steep. Colombo takes out his money and hands it to the taxi driver. "Thanks for the ride."

The cab driver smiles and says, "Enjoy your party."

Colombo exits the cab, walks up the driveway, and passes the other district heads' cars. He knocks on the door three times and admires the expensive watch on his wrist as he does.

Leo is in the backyard drinking whiskey with Antonio. Raymond and Antonio were the best of friends, which is why Leo and Mario are, for the most part. Antonio is telling Leo of his father. "So, we told the bartender to give the girl two martinis from us. Let me remind you, Raymond had just received his steak from the waiter. Anyway, the girls came up to us, and we knew it was game time."

"Wait, when did you say this was?" Leo asks.

"I remember him going out because he was so stressed out about your gig failing. So, about four to six months ago. Anyway, they came up to us and told us how sweet we are and all of that other horseshit. When Raymond asked if he could take them back home, the girl said no. Raymond is caught off guard, so he asks why. Do you know what she says? You're too old."

Leo starts to laugh his ass off after hearing about how his terrible father was turned down for being too old. "I bet he didn't take that too well," Leo says.

"Way to spoil the climax. Do you want to know what he did? He grabbed the steak and chucked it at her face, and it was a T-bone! We ran out of there like inmates busting out of prison."

Leo is laughing over the hysterical story so much that he's crying, so is Antonio. "Oh boy, your father was quite a character. Nobody liked him because of how cruel he could be, but not me. I saw through that bullshit and saw a good man. When I find out who did that shit to him, that person is as good as dead."

"Did what?" Leo asks.

"You know what I'm talking about; whoever killed him."

"Killed him? Antonio, Raymond fell off of the balcony. He was found with an open bottle of whiskey and a cigar. He just slipped."

"Believe what you want, but your father isn't that foolish. This was a hit, and I can't be convinced otherwise. The only thing I ponder is why one would put a hit on Raymond. He was a very neutral man, and he never had bad blood with anybody." Antonio explains.

"Antonio, I can assure you that he passed on his own," Leo says with his hand on his father's dear friend's shoulder.

"Between the two of us, I think it was one of Bruno's men."

Leo downs the rest of his drink and says, "Antonio, it wasn't a hit. Tread lightly on such matters."

Marco approaches all of the district heads at the party, even Leo. He tells them about how he found the cocaine in the cigar box. The red flag with the cocaine isn't the fact that he's jacked up on it, even though that's part of the problem for Leo personally. The red flag is how he hid the stash so terribly. With a police officer and many district muggles in the house, that's a huge security alert.

Marco and the heads approach Noah on the couch; they are standing so intimidatingly. Marco smirks and says, "Noah, a little word in your garage?"

Noah looks around at his fellow district heads without a clue what this word Marco wants to have may be about, and then he looks at his brother, who stands tall amongst the men as he nods his head. "What is this in reference to?" Noah asks as he gulps.

Marco smirks again and reaches into his back pocket, and takes out the box of Glens. Noah acknowledges the situation and sighs. He's embarrassed, which is a scarce feeling for Noah. He thinks to himself, shit, they know.

Noah gets up on his feet and nods, knowing that there's no way out of this situation. He makes his way through his house as the men follow along. As Noah walks, he wonders what the consequences will be this time. He knows it won't lead to a hit because of all the witnesses; that is obvious.

Noah gets to the garage door and opens it up. The heads enter the garage, and the last one to enter, Colombo, locks the door. Noah fears what may follow this chain of events. It starts with Marco walking up to Noah with the box and saying, "I've met a lot of people, but I've never met someone as stupid as you."

"What the fuck are you trying to say? How am I stupid?" Noah asks.

"Let me ask you something. What does your father-in-law do for work? I'll answer for you... he's a cop. A cop that hates your guts. A cop whose favorite cigar brand could be Glens. A cop who could've found your fucking coke and arrested your ass!" Marco shouts.

"Jesus Christ, would you keep your fucking voice down? You're so worried that he'll find my stash, and here you are shouting as if you're at a rally." Noah barks.

"I don't want to hear shit from you. This isn't your first slip. The failed gig, the bailing on the meetings, the lack of cooperation with the recession, the lack of cooperation with Abruzzo, and now you're getting sloppy. There's no room for slop in this business, and as a matter of fact, there's no room for the both of us in the same business." Marco rants.

Noah starts to cry, feeling like a total failure and giving the district heads a reason to poke him around. He rubs his hands on his forehead, and he starts his spiel: "It started as a part of a deal, Leo can vouch. I asked for a coke, and I wanted cola. They gave me cocaine, and I was under pressure. I did what I had to do to seal the deal, and it worked. I liked the feeling of power, so I went back for more to Colombo."

Leo puts two and two together and then concludes why he was in the club that one night when he got those wings at midnight. "Pull yourself together. Stop crying." Leo says

Noah snaps and shouts, "My God! I'm sorry that I'm such a fucking embarrassment!"

"Yeah, you know what? Apology unaccepted! I carry the weight of our district; I make things happen. All you do is give them reasons to terminate our partnership."

Sinful and Healing, both hurting during this rampage, team up for once to fight back. "You just found out that your brother is a cocaine addict, and you're worried about a fucking partnership? Are you fucking serious?"

"I am! If you want to kill yourself with these fucking drugs, go ahead. See how much I care." Leo says.

"The point is that we don't want you involved with us anymore. We don't trust you." Mario says as he takes out a cigar.

"You don't trust me?" Noah asks, feeling offended and just downright pissed off.

"You're not a team player. It makes us think of rats." Robert says.

"A rat? What the fuck have I done to be a rat?"

"You may not be a rat just yet, but you certainly share the same qualities." Robert points out.

Mario puffs on his cigar and says to Noah, who is on his knees crying, "Noah, I highly suggest that you resign. Do I have to make myself clear, or do you get what I'm implying?"

Noah wipes off his tears for just a moment to say, "Give me another chance. I've had so much going on in my life right now with the whole baby thing. Please!"

"Noah, we all have lives outside of our districts. If everybody were to let their stumbling blocks get in the way of everything, nothing would ever get done." Marco says.

"We'll let you be alone. We're sorry that it didn't work out, I hope you know that." Mario says in an attempt to console his friend's brother.

Marco throws the bag of cocaine at Noah and says, "Keep it."

The men make their way out of the garage, and they unlock the door and exit one at a time. Before Colombo exits, Noah cries, "Colombo! Jimmy!"

Colombo sighs and turns back to Noah without saying a word. "I thought we were friends." Noah lets out.

Feeling tribulations like never before, Colombo acts tough and slams the door shut, leaving Noah alone in the garage with his depression.

Mario stops walking and puts his hand on Leo's shoulder; the other heads proceed and make their way to the backyard. Leo's nose is a little runny, and his eyes are a bit red. "Hey, brighten up. That was necessary; you know that. You did what was not only best for us but him. You ought to know that your brother in this business is a disaster waiting to happen." Mario says.

"I know. I'm just a little worried, that's all." Leo says.

"Isn't this what you always wanted?" Mario asks.

Leo thinks about that question. Isn't this what I always wanted? I mean, you were so pissed off in the beginning when Raymond just made you a co-head, and you were so fucking offended, remember that? But Leo, you fucked over your brother. He's in there crying his eyes out.

"I guess this is an aspect of what I always wanted. I don't know; I just wish I didn't have to leave him in the dust."

Normally, a district head would leave it at that. But Mario and Leo are pals, and you don't walk out on your pals. "I may not be the sharpest, but I do know some stuff. For example, I've learned that no dream ever perfectly unfolds. C'mon, let's grab a drink."

Leo feels sick to his stomach. Even a single drop of booze in his system will send him over the brink and make him hurl his last two meals. He wipes the tear that's trying to fall down his face before it does, and then he hugs his friend. Leo is hugging Mario and for once…after all of the gunshots, after all of the money recessions, after all of the murders, after all of the betrayal, after all of the heartbreaks…for once, it wasn't two district heads hugging, but friends.

The barbecue is dead, and all of the guests, except for Molly's family, have left. Noah just lays down on the couch and stares at the ceiling. Nathan and Adam go up to Noah and ask, "Are you just going to lay there? We were hoping to watch a boxing match."

Noah rubs his eyes and says, "Kicking me off of my couch? Sounds about right. Whatever, nothing matters anymore."

Noah gets up from the couch before his arrogant brother-in-law, or his piece of shit father-in-law can say a word. They sit down on the couch and wonder what just happened with Noah.

Noah walks to the bathroom and passes his wife and his mother-in-law in the kitchen. He goes into the bathroom and yanks out his bag of cocaine. Instead of dumping out a smaller amount of cocaine to draw two lines, he dumps the whole load.

He takes out the credit card that he uses to spend his blood money and draws one line at first. No straw? Doesn't matter. He snorts the line quickly and then moves on to make the next. *Snnnnifffff.* Done!

The following line is longer, and an additional line accompanies it on its right side. *Snnnnifffff.* Noah scurries to the next line. *Snnnnifffff.*

Noah feels so energized, so empowered, so concentrated. He can hear the clock in the living room tick, tick, tick, tick. His vision is so clear; he can read the fine print on the shampoo bottle that's in the shower. He's so energized; he can do a marathon and make it back home in time to watch tonight's episode of *Magnificent Massacres.*

In conclusion, Noah feels like he has enough of everything to do pretty much anything in a matter of minutes. However, this feeling of power doesn't match the feeling of depression that dominates his mindset.

He's not sad about not being in the business. He's completely devastated over the number of sacrifices he made for the business. He nearly ruined his marriage; he slapped his wife, watched his brother kill his father, and for what? He's out, and it's all over for him.

He almost lost everything over a dumb job that he didn't even want. When he looks into the mirror, he doesn't see Raymond or any other hallucination, and he sees himself and despises the view.

He asks himself questions like, *what kind of husband are you? What kind of father are you? What kind of being do you identify yourself with because it's not human. I know that much. You don't deserve a wife and son; you deserve to fucking die!*

Noah, mainly Sinful, comes to an ultimate decision. First, he swipes all of the cocaine off the counter onto his hand and drops it into the toilet, and he flushes and watches his poison sink.

Next, he splashes cold water on his face and feels what he imagines getting punched in the face with water from Antarctica feels like physically.

He storms out of the bathroom and passes the kitchen again. Molly watches her frantic husband make his way to the staircase and asks, "Honey, should I fix you something to eat?"

Noah stops walking and stares at his gorgeous wife. He cries on the inside and lets out the words, "No thanks."

"Oh, ok. I love you."

Noah grasps the railing as if he's holding onto a handrail on Ahab's ship while it sinks. "I love you so much," Noah says as he holds back a whole gallon of tears.

"Are you ok?" Maya asks.

Dodging the question, Noah says, "You know what, I'm going to my office for a bit. I'd appreciate it if nobody disturbed me."

Noah starts to walk upstairs with a plan that'll lead to his inescapable demise. The commute from the bottom of the staircase to the top feels faster than it ever has before.

He enters his office and grabs a black pen from his cup of utensils. He slides a few sheets of paper from a large stack and writes on the top left corner:

Dear Molly,

He thinks to himself; *these pricks want a rat? I'll give them a rat.*

Leo sits at a table in a diner with Henrietta and tells her about everything. "I don't know what to do. I feel like I let him down."

"In a way, you did. However, you did the smart thing. He was a mess, so don't beat yourself up." Henrietta says.

Leo sits there with his milkshake and wonders what he can do to better this situation. Noah's left with nowhere to go; he didn't finish college, and Leo doesn't like that at all. He wonders, what can I do? What can I do?

"What are his interests?" Henrietta asks.

"Well, he was planning on business school. But plans changed when Molly got pregnant, and then the district opportunity presented itself."

"Well, there you go. Pay for Noah to go to business school. He can make something of himself."

Leo smiles at his girlfriend and leans over to kiss her on the forehead. "You're so fucking smart. That's a great idea! Why the fuck didn't I think of that?"

Henrietta smiles and digs into her burger. "I think I'm just going to do that. It works out perfectly, don't you think?" Leo says.

"I suggested it for a reason," Henrietta says with a mouth full of beef, cheese, and bun.

"You know what, I'm going to drive down there and tell him. Do you need cab fare?"

"Yes, please. What time do you think you'll be home by?"

"Depends on if he wants celebratory drinks. Hopefully, not much more than an hour by the time you get home. The key is under the mat." Leo says as he takes ten bucks out of his wallet and hands it to her.

Noah finishes his letter in his office, and it only takes him five minutes. When you're jacked up on cocaine and know exactly what you want to say, you express yourself very quickly.

He rearranges his desk lamp, so the light shines directly on the letter. He kisses his index and middle finger and then presses them onto the paper.

He moves out of the office and shuts the door. Noah enters his bedroom and walks over to the crib. He looks at his son, kisses his own hand, and then presses it onto his son's forehead.

He moves across the room and grabs the rope that he and Molly were planning on using for a porch swing outside. He curls it up and starts to carry it out of the room and to the garage.

He maneuvers his way around the house so he can enter the garage without anybody seeing. He grabs a stool from the corner of his garage and moves it to the center.

He stands up on the stool and ties the rope to the metal bar above him. He makes himself a noose and prepares himself for the journey from Earth to hell.

He shuts his eyes for a moment to process the situation. *Do you want to do this? There's no going back. If this turns out to be a mistake, it'll be the mistake of all errors. Do we want to risk such odds? What do you have for you here? No matter how nice you act, you'll never be the man for Molly. No matter how wealthy you are, you can never provide for your son in the ways he needs. All you do is fuck Shit up. Your brother hates you, your father hates you, your father-in-law hates you, and so does your brother. What if you go to hell? You're a good guy deep down; I don't think you will. But, what if you do? What if we sink right to the bottom of hell? This is fucking crazy. You don't want to die. This is all just an act. Open your fucking eyes; you have it better than most.*

153

When Noah opens his eyes, he sees Raymond. No mirror, just Raymond with a smile. "Well, well, well. Look at how far you've come."

"Don't get any ideas. I'm not going through with this. I was just going a bit crazy; we all do."

"Oh, sure. When I used to get crazy, I'd drink a little too much booze. When you get crazy, you write a suicide note that rats out all of the district heads. You are trying to destroy an empire that myself and many others have worked so hard to build."

"What has this business done for me? What good has come from this?" Noah asks.

"Do you know why I gave you a position in my district? Because I wanted to get back at Leo for all of those years of kissing my ass. Never for a second did I give you such a position because I thought you deserved it, not once. You're just going to let yourself crash just like how you let Leo kill me?"

"I used to feel that way. I used to feel like I let Leo kill you. But really, you let him kill you. You never planned on killing us, and I think Leo knew that. You could've seen Leo's hit from a mile away, and you could've prevented it successfully. But no. You knew it was either you get killed, or you retire, and you didn't want to retire, so you let Leo do what he did." Noah rants, unfolding a mystery that Raymond figured was unsolvable.

"Wow, you hit the hammer on the nail. You have some fucking nerve. In my eyes, you're still a coward with a big mouth. Every time I've come to you, I've hidden behind glass, and I'm not hiding behind anything now. Take your best shot, you fucking lousy excuse of a son, a sorry excuse for a husband, and a sad excuse for a man." Raymond says with a smile.

Noah loses all of his senses at once and charges after his father, leading to him falling off of the stool that was the only thing preventing him from hanging to death.

Noah tries to swing his feet back onto the stool or get himself out of the noose. As he tries, he watches his father stand in front of him and laugh hysterically. Raymond claps his hand and smokes his cigar at the sight of his son hanging. Sinful and Healing both turn into Dying. Raymond sits down on his chair and puts out his cigar, and this hallucination Noah has of his father starts to fade away. He snaps out of his delusion just to enter a sane mindset that he will live out the last seconds of his life with.

He thinks to himself; *this can't be the end. I'm too young to reach the end of the line. I'm too young to see the light at the end of the tunnel. My poor wife. My poor son. My brother.* Noah wishes for the metal bar holding the rope to collapse.

Noah's last sight is a small bike. This is the small bike his father taught him to ride. He thinks, *I've lucked out in life before, so maybe I'll–*

Leo walks up the steps of the house and knocks on the door; he anxiously awaits an answer. He's hoping that his brother will take comfort in this visit. Molly answers the door and sees her brother-in-law stand tall and ecstatic. "Hey Molly, can I speak with Noah?" Leo asks.

"Sure. He's up in his office. What brings you back?" Molly asks as she hugs Leo and kisses him on the cheek.

"I have news that I think he'll like," Leo answers.

Leo skips the rest of the casualties with his sister-in-law and runs upstairs to Noah's office. He enters and spots the letter. It appears to be like the holy grail with the way the lamp lights it up.

He picks up the letter and begins to read the letter:

Dear Molly,

If you're reading this and don't know why, go down to the garage, and you'll find me dead. There's no easy way to write such a letter, but I can imagine that it's probably harder to read this than write it out. I've never been too good at goodbyes, so I guess I won't be very good with this. I just want you to know this has nothing to do with you and everything to do with me. I'm not the husband or father you need in your life or our son's. I love you both so much, and you guys make it impossible to do this. I'm just not fit for this life. The truth is I'm a criminal. I'm involved with something called a district, and there are several. The Santino District, the Russo District, the Alfredo District, the Bruno District, the Colombo District, and now the Abruzzo District combine to make one extensive partnership. Leo and I run the Santino District. We do distribution. Russo does deliveries. Alfredo does the storage of things that you don't want cops to find with a search warrant. Bruno does hits, as in killing people. Colombo sells drugs, some of which I purchase. Abruzzo sells guns. I want you to get this letter and information into the hands of the feds. The names of these men are Leonardo Santino, Marco Russo, Mario Alfredo, Robert Jr. Bruno, Jimmy Jr. Colombo, Peter Abruzzo. These men have inherited these districts through their fathers. I'm going out in such a way because I can't do jail time. And even though this would qualify me as an informant and put me under the WPP, I don't want to ruin your life. I wouldn't want that for you and our child. I can't go to jail because I can't even imagine the image of you or Nathan seeing me behind bars. I don't feel like I do anything but kill myself mentally every day of every week of the year. Again, I love you and Nathan more than I love anything else in this world. Again, I'm not good at goodbyes. I don't know what else to say. I do ask that you make my absence from Nathan's life seem reasonable. Make him think I was a good guy. If that's too much to ask for, then that's fair enough. I love you. I guess there's nothing left for me to do but something insane for the last time. I love you.

Sincerely,

Noah

Leo shoves the note into his back pocket and says, "Shit! Noah!"

Before he can do anything, he hears a scream from downstairs. Leo rushes down the large set of stairs and sees Nathan and Adam running towards the garage where the girls already are as they look at Noah hanging dead from the ceiling.

Leo sees this disaster and forgets about everything else, even Henrietta. "No! What the fuck happened?" Leo cries as he runs towards Molly, who is holding Noah's dangling body.

Molly starts bawling her eyes out and says, "I just wanted to see if the cabinet in the garage had the pictures my mom wanted to see, and there he was."

Leo stares at his dead brother, who is dangling on a rope meant for his son's leisure. He takes full responsibility but keeps that to himself. He decides that the suicide letter he has stuffed in his pocket will stay put until he gets home and gets the chance to burn it entirely.

Leo runs to the body, holds it for dear life, and shouts, "Noah, not you! Not my brother! You're the only brother I have! You're the only brother I want! I'm sorry! I'm sorry for all of the times I called you stupid! I'm sorry for the times where we fought! I'm sorry for hitting you that one time! I love you, Noah! I never said it to you, but I'm saying it to you now! I love you! Not my boy! Not my brother! Noah, I'm so sorry! I'm sorry for pushing you over the edge sometimes! I'm sorry that I treated you like shit! I'm sorry Raymond treated you like shit! I'm sorry for everything! I love you, Noah! I never said it to you, but I'm saying it to you now! I love you!"

Leo falls to the ground in tears and bangs his fist onto the floor as if the ground caused this incident. "Fuck!" Leo lets out.

At the wake, Leo stands to the side of Molly, who holds baby Nathan in her arms. Mrs. Bambino from the diner comes up to Leo and says, "This is terrible. I'm so sorry for this.".

Mrs. Bambino hugs him and Leo says into the old lady's ear, "He just loved you. It means a lot to him and me that you came today."

"How could I not?" Mrs. Bambino says, wrapping things up with Leo so she can apologize to Molly for her loss.

Next up to bat are the district heads who Leo didn't want to see. Pete shakes hands with Leo and throws in a little pat on the back. "I'm sorry for your loss."

Leo nods, and Pete moves along to Molly, leaving Colombo next in line. "I'm disappointed with the way I left off with Noah. He was a good guy, and to tell you the truth, I feel partially responsible for the dark path he went down."

"Don't beat yourself up; we all make our own decisions at the end of the day." Leo insists.

Bruno shakes hands with Leo, and the two do an awkward hug kind of thing. "Sorry, pal."

Leo smiles, and then Robert walks off. Mario goes up to Leo, and the two immediately hug. The tight embrace somewhat comforts Leo, who feels empty inside. "I hate that this happened, and I can't tell you enough. No matter what I may have said, he was a good kid."

"Thanks, I appreciate that. Thanks for coming." Leo says as the two stop hugging.

Last and least, Marco walks up to Leo, and the two shake hands. "Sorry for your loss. A real bummer, huh?"

"This is a bummer, I agree," Leo says, a little bit annoyed.

"Well, chin up, pal. We have work tomorrow." Marco says as he gently slaps Leo in the face a couple of times.

Leo pauses for a moment and thinks about that: we have work tomorrow. Leo realizes that he doesn't just have work tomorrow, but every day for the rest of his life. In the district business, you either go out voluntarily or involuntarily. You either act smart and retire when you see the end coming near, or you take your precious time and get hit.

In 1979, Raymond Santino had a tough choice to make. On the one hand, he can either step down from his district like the other heads and spend the rest of his life regretting his retirement. On the other hand, he

ABOUT THE AUTHOR

M. B. Heywood is the author of various stories in the world of the Vaporous Realms. These include several snippet series on the Vaporous Realms Substack, multiple Songs of the Vaporous Realms series on Vella, and the Tales of the Vaporous Realms novellas, of which this is the first. Heywood also develops tabletop gaming resources for the Vaporous Realms at War.

In our world, he is a wandering storyteller and scribe for hire, hailing from a little ways south of the Mason-Dixon. He loves his Lord, his wife and youngins, their kith and kin, coffee and pie, epic fantasy, historical anecdotes, miniature models, and in spite of himself, the cat.

Keep up with the latest from M. B. Heywood at www.VaporousRealms.com and the Vaporous Realms Substack. Follow generations of adventurers across the Vaporous Realms story-cycles: Dustsong, Eastsong, Northsong, Southsong, and Westsong! The tale of Len and his companions will continue with *Kaelii the Defiant* and *Egwae the Arbiter*.

Made in United States
Troutdale, OR
09/28/2023

13262422R00096

can let his son take his own life so that he can leave life without stepping down like a coward.

Leo stands in the middle of that funeral staring at his fellow district heads as they chat amongst themselves. He realizes that these are the pricks that he will spend the rest of his life dealing with all of the time. When somebody rubs Leo the wrong way or makes him feel unsafe, it's Bruno who he'll go to for protection. Whenever a client wants a gun, it's Abruzzo he'll be using. When he needs a delivery, Marco will be behind the wheel or at least plan for somebody else to do the job. When he needs to ship drugs to that club in Jersey, Colombo will be supplying. When he wants a laugh and a good time, it's Mario he'll be clinking whiskey glasses with at his pizza place. He has no easy exits in this business, but that's the life of a district head.

THE END